"Long! You son of a bitch . . ."

The lean man reached for both his guns at once.

Longarm reacted without taking time to think about it. His Colt came out and he pointed instinctively at the man's gut, at the same time dropping into a crouch. The flat, hammering roar of Longarm's .45 filled the low-ceilinged saloon, and a cloud of white gun smoke billowed out from his muzzle.

The lean man looked down where a splash of bright blood was beginning to stain the front of his shirt. "Damn . . ." He tried to raise his pistols, but they seemed too heavy a burden "Damn you," he managed. Then he slowly toppled forward into the sawdust and the spit that covered the saloon floor.

Longarm took a step toward the dying man—but froze in place at the ominous *cla-clack* sound of a pistol being cocked behind his back . . .

TABOR EVANS

LONGARM

AND THE TINY THIEF

JOVE BOOKS, NEW YORK

THE BERKLEY PUBLISHING GROUP
Published by the Penguin Group
Penguin Group (USA) Inc.
375 Hudson Street, New York, New York 10014, USA
Penguin Group (Canada), 90 Eglinton Avenue East, Suite 700, Toronto, Ontario M4P 2Y3, Canada
(a division of Pearson Penguin Canada Inc.)
Penguin Books Ltd., 80 Strand, London WC2R 0RL, England
Penguin Group Ireland, 25 St. Stephen's Green, Dublin 2, Ireland (a division of Penguin Books Ltd.)
Penguin Group (Australia), 250 Camberwell Road, Camberwell, Victoria 3124, Australia
(a division of Pearson Australia Group Pty. Ltd.)
Penguin Books India Pvt. Ltd., 11 Community Centre, Panchsheel Park, New Delhi—110 017, India
Penguin Group (NZ), 67 Apollo Drive, Rosedale, North Shore 0632, New Zealand
(a division of Pearson New Zealand Ltd.)
Penguin Books (South Africa) (Pty.) Ltd., 24 Sturdee Avenue, Rosebank, Johannesburg 2196,
South Africa

Penguin Books Ltd., Registered Offices: 80 Strand, London WC2R 0RL, England

This is a work of fiction. Names, characters, places, and incidents either are the product of the author's imagination or are used fictitiously, and any resemblance to actual persons, living or dead, business establishments, events, or locales is entirely coincidental.

LONGARM AND THE TINY THIEF

A Jove Book / published by arrangement with the author

PRINTING HISTORY
Jove edition / April 2008

ISBN: 978-0-515-14447-5

JOVE®
Jove Books are published by The Berkley Publishing Group,
a division of Penguin Group (USA) Inc.,
375 Hudson Street, New York, New York 10014.
JOVE is a registered trademark of Penguin Group (USA) Inc.
The "J" design is a trademark belonging to Penguin Group (USA) Inc.

PRINTED IN THE UNITED STATES OF AMERICA

10 9 8 7 6 5 4 3 2 1

Chapter 1

Longarm's boot heels struck hollowly on the boardwalk that stretched across the front of the little mercantile. Behind him he heard the jehu call, "Twenty minutes, folks. If you ain't aboard in twenty minutes, we'll go on without you. Trust me 'bout this."

Most of Longarm's fellow passengers were headed west. Dreaming the golden dreams more than likely. He only wanted to make a connection back to Denver. For the past three weeks he had been standing ready to give testimony in a mail robbery case—testimony that was never required, but the prosecutor was taking no chances and refused to relieve Marshal William Vail's best deputy until the last dog was hung, or in this case jailed for twelve and a half to twenty years—and after that much sheer boredom. Longarm was more than ready to get back to his next assignment.

The others, a collection of drummers pretending to be businessmen and whores pretending to be respectable, headed for a café in . . . he had no idea what town he was in. Riding inside that rocking, creaking, miserable coach, he tended to lose track of things. While his fellow passengers grabbed pie and coffee, Longarm wanted to replenish

1

his supply of cheroots. He'd run out nearly a week ago and had been making do with rum crooks ever since.

He entered the mercantile and blinked in the deep shade of the indoors. Stepping to the side, he removed his flat-crowned brown Stetson and resettled it on his head as a pretext to give his eyes a moment to adjust after the bright sunlight outside.

A shaft of golden sunlight lanced through the skylight over the mercantile door. Specks of dust danced and floated in the light.

A gent in sleeve garters and eyeshades stood behind the counter. Over by the side windows, a redheaded kid was standing by a display case.

"Can I help you, mister?" the proprietor asked.

"I surely hope so," Longarm told him. "Got any cheroots? Pale panatelas would do, but I tend t' favor the cheroots."

"I have some, friend, but they come dear. Two for a penny, never mind that they're so small."

Longarm grunted unhappily, but he reached into his pocket and pulled out a nickel, reached again and came up with a penny. "I'll have ten of your cheroots an' a penny's worth o' matches, please."

"Yes, sir. Give me just a minute to fetch them. I keep them in a humidor."

Longarm nodded and idly turned to survey the interior of the place while he waited.

A tall man, several inches over six feet in height, Custis Long was a study in brown. Brown corduroy trousers, brown calfskin vest with a chain across his flat belly, black string tie, and black knee-high stovepipe cavalry boots. His brown coat was outside lying on the seat of the McCormick Express Company coach.

He had a huge sweep of brown mustache, a deep tan, and eyes that could be warm and caring one moment or hard as steel the next.

He wore a black gunbelt high on his waist, his double-action .44 rigged for a cross-draw. One end of his watch chain was attached to a railroad-quality Ingersoll stem-wind watch, the other to a single-shot derringer. Both were tools that he considered useful to his trade as a deputy United States marshal.

"There you are, sir. Is there anything else?"

"For what it's worth," Longarm said softly, "the boy over there is stealing you blind."

"What? Why, the little son of a bitch. Wait till I get my hands on him," the proprietor declared.

"Wait a second there, neighbor," Longarm said. "Let me put a proper scare into him." He demonstrated what he meant by reaching for his badge to show the kid, then remembered too late that his wallet and badge were in the inside pocket of his corduroy coat, still inside the coach.

Not that he really needed a badge to impress a ten-year-old kid, he figured. Longarm shrugged off the inconvenience and sauntered down the aisle to the counter where the boy was standing, seeming to pay no attention to either Longarm or the storekeeper.

"Say, boy, d'you got money to pay for all that truck you've stuffed inside your shirt an' down your pant legs?" Longarm boomed. "I'm a deputy U.S. marshal, and I believe I've caught a thief red-handed."

The kid whirled around and peered wide-eyed up at this stranger who suddenly accosted him. "I . . . I . . . oh, no."

The boy turned bug-eyed and pale and stammered something Longarm could not understand.

"Give it up, kid," he snapped, as hard and cold as he could manage. His hope was to so thoroughly frighten the boy that any further thought of stealing would practically make him wet himself.

The boy stared soundlessly for a moment.

Longarm remembered how starkly the kid's freckles stood out atop the pale face. Remembered the china blue eyes. The bright red hair. The obvious fear.

3

What he did not remember, then or ever, was the kid's hand flashing.

Or the knife blade that glanced off the tough leather of Longarm's gunbelt and pierced his belly.

Under the circumstances that seemed strange, but Longarm never had any recollection of it at all.

Chapter 2

The next thing Longarm became aware of was a musty, stale odor that seemed to surround him. He puzzled on that for what felt like a very long time before he worked out—slowly and with great difficulty—that the odor came from a mattress and that he was in fact lying on it.

He was in a bed. In a room he had never seen before. There was a cheap floral-print paper on the walls. The one window was covered with sheets of yellowed newspaper pasted over . . . he studied on it and decided the window was glazed with slabs of wood, not glass. Whoever owned the place was what might be called frugal.

Longarm was completely naked, he discovered, except for a linen bandage wrapped around his midsection and a thin muslin sheet draped over him. He had no idea why that should be so, but his belly hurt like a sonuvabitch. He badly needed a shave.

Day turned to night and back to day again. He knew he was missing significant chunks of time there, but he did not particularly care. That seemed quite unimportant. Sometime the next day—late morning, he judged—he was awake when a man came into the room carrying a tray with a cup on it. From the cup arose the most tantalizingly wonderful

5

scent Longarm ever smelled. Chicken broth. He was sure of it. His gut rumbled and his mouth began to water.

The man grunted. "You're awake now."

Longarm nodded. "I . . . I . . . yeah. A little." He yawned. "Sleepy."

"Shit, mister, you been sleeping four days already. A body would think you'd be rested by now."

"Sorry, I . . . what happened anyhow?"

"You was stabbed. Damned thief, a little kid too, up and stabbed you. Tried to cut your guts out, but Jason . . . he runs the store you was in at the time . . . Jason says you moved awful fast and damn near got out of the way of the knife. Says as it was, the blade went in at an angle and must've missed your bowels, or else by now you'd be laying in that bed howling with pain and begging for somebody to shoot you to make it stop. Says it seems strange that a man will put a horse out of its misery but not a fellow man. Which, I suppose, is neither here nor there far as you're concerned."

"Thank goodness," Longarm mumbled. "If the blade didn't do all that much damage, how come I'm layin' here?"

"Shock. Jason said you went into what he called shock."

"Jason is a doctor too?"

"No, but he assisted the doctors in surgery back during the war." The fellow shook his head admiringly and smiled. "Now if you want an arm or a leg taken off, Jason's your man to do it. He says many a time when the wounded kept coming and the docs couldn't keep up, they'd turn the routine cases over to the assistants. Says he couldn't begin to recall how many limbs he's cut off." The smile turned into a grin. "Says in your case he wanted to amputate, but he couldn't figure out which half to save and which to throw away. So he decided to see could he save the whole thing."

"Reckon I'll have t' thank this Jason person next time I see him," Longarm said.

"Oh, he'll be by to check on you after he closes the store this evening. He comes often as he can."

"Then who are you, if you don't mind my askin', and where am I?"

"My name is Sluter. Abner Payne Sluter if you want the long of it. And I am the station manager . . . also chief hostler, freight agent, ticket seller, and floor sweeper . . . for the McCormick Express Company. I'm also the closest thing we got to having law hereabouts. Some of the townsfolk named me constable and pinned a badge on my chest. When you were stabbed, it just seemed logical for me to take you in. Sort of my responsibility if you see what I mean."

"Yeah, I . . . where's my stuff? I had all my stuff on that stage."

"The agent in Denver noticed your 'stuff,' as you call it, still on the coach when everyone else got off at the end of the run. Someone told him about you being hurt here, so he turned it around and sent it back. Your stuff is in that wardrobe right over there."

"Thanks. Thank you very much." Not that there was so very much stuff involved. Since the trip had just been a matter of giving courtroom testimony, Longarm's McClellan saddle and Winchester carbine were in his boardinghouse room back home in Denver. He would be wanting his coat, though, with his deputy's wallet hopefully still in it, and his carpetbag with a change of clothing. The things he had been wearing when he got here were probably bloody and ruined now.

"Could I . . . do you think I could . . . ?" He lifted his chin and used it to point toward the tray his benefactor still held and to the cup of chicken broth on it.

"Oh!" The fellow grinned again. "I swear, I'd forget my own butt if it wasn't nailed in place."

He sat down on the edge of the bed and carefully propped some musty pillows behind the patient to raise Longarm's head a little, then held the cup so Longarm could drink.

Longarm was fairly sure he had never in his life tasted anything half so fine as that chicken broth.

"Good?"

"Mmm-hmm."

"More?"

"Mmm-hmm."

By the time he was halfway through the broth, his eyes were dropping closed. There were questions he wanted to ask. What happened to the kid? Where the hell was he?

His questions would simply have to wait, though. He was asleep again long before the helpful station agent wiped his mouth and tugged the sheet up under his chin.

Chapter 3

"I think you should stay in bed a few more days," the former surgeon's assistant admonished.

"Thank you for your concern, Mr. Bradley, but I'm feeling better now." He grinned. "Goin' crazy from lyin' in bed like that with nothing t' do but think." The grin became all the larger. "Truth is, Jason, I ain't accustomed to this thinking business. Reckon it would take some getting used to."

Longarm winced when he bent over to grab the mule ears on his boot so he could pull it on. He paused for a moment, then bent down and got the other boot on without any display of pain.

"Careful," Bradley warned. "The infection that laid you low has subsided, but I don't say it can't come back. You mustn't try to travel yet. Not on horseback and not bouncing around in the back of a stagecoach either. Give yourself some time to heal."

"I have t' get back to Denver, Jason."

"Of course you do, but I suspect you would rather go back on a coach seat instead of in a box. If you tear that cut open and become infected again, the sepsis could well kill you. Frankly, I am surprised it didn't kill you already." The storekeeper smiled. "You have the constitution of a bull moose."

"Yeah, everybody tells me that." Longarm buckled his gunbelt in place and winced again. That hurt like hell. Maybe Jason was right about him laying low for a few more days. The wire from his boss, U.S. Marshal Billy Vail, told him to take as much time as he needed for his recovery. Maybe he should stay here in Roy's Crossing just a little longer.

It surprised him how weak and shaky his legs were. Jason assured him that was only temporary, but it worried him nonetheless.

"If you think you're going to fall," Jason said, "grab hold of me. I'll support you."

"How far are we goin'?" Longarm asked.

"The café is just across the street."

"An' I can have real food for a change?"

Jason laughed. "Yes, you can have real food."

"Good 'cause when I shaved this morning, I seen some o' that oatmeal o' yours leaking outa my right ear."

"That wasn't oatmeal, Longarm, that was what passes for brains in your thick head."

"Huh. Sharp enough t' whip your sorry ass at checkers, ain't I?"

"Lucky enough, you mean."

"You call it luck. Me, I call it skill."

Longarm tottered slowly outdoors and just stood there for a few moments, enjoying the sensation of being surrounded by moving air and an open sky.

"Are you all right?" Jason asked, close at his side.

"Yeah. Better'n ever." He meant that too. "Better'n ever."

"The café is right over there. Do you think you're up to walking that far?"

"Just stand back, man, an' don't get between me an' that steak you promised."

"All right, let's go."

Half an hour later, his belly full and feeling more content

than he had in quite some time, Longarm asked, "Where's your jail, Jason?"

"We don't have a proper jail in the place. Hell, we don't have a proper town to put a jail in, just like we don't have a proper town marshal's office."

"I thought you said you locked up that boy that stabbed me."

"I said exactly that. But we don't have a jail to lock him into. The kid is in chains over in the express company's barn."

"For Pete's sake, Jason!" Longarm blurted. "You've had the boy in chains for all this time?"

Jason shrugged. "At first we were waiting to see if you died, in which case we would've been charging him with murder. Then you began to improve, and by then we were used to having him there. Besides, the little bastard is a real hard case. He won't even tell us his name, much less where he is from or who his folks are. We figure we'll just keep him right there where he is until the circuit judge comes through again."

"An' when will that be?"

"Late next month. Maybe. Depending on how his schedule is in the meantime. We aren't exactly high on anybody's list of priorities for services of any sort. Including law enforcement."

"You can't keep a child chained up forever," Longarm said.

"Maybe not, but there's times when it seems a good idea."

"I want to see him. Have a talk with him."

"I'll take you over there when you're up to a little more walking. Not now. This is far enough for your first time out."

"You should've been a doctor, Jason."

From the storekeeper's reaction, Longarm realized he

had struck a nerve there. An unpleasant one. Something had kept Bradley from following up on his wartime experiences and becoming a physician in his own right. Something unpleasant, judging from the bleak and stricken look on the man's face when Longarm made that seemingly simple statement.

"Sorry," Longarm mumbled.

Bradley forced a smile. "Tomorrow," he said. "I'll take you out to the barn tomorrow."

Longarm nodded and laid a coin down to pay for their meal. Damn, but it felt good to be out again. But the truth was that just walking across the street had worn him out. He would be glad to get back into bed again now.

Chapter 4

Payne Sluter's house, where Longarm was staying, was at the opposite end of the town from the express company office where Sluter worked. Behind that was the barn where the boy was being held awaiting trial. Longarm thought there must be some sort of natural law about that: Whatever is the most difficult and most inconvenient is the way things turn out to be. Guaranteed.

Not that there was so very much "town" to get between the two. Roy's Crossing did not seem large enough to support more than one stray cat at a time. The few businesses made their living from farms and a ranch or two in the surrounding vicinity. Longarm doubted there were more than a couple dozen folks who lived in the place.

He sat on the porch at the front of Sluter's house and had a smoke. Sluter was at work at the express company and Jason Bradley was tending his store. Those two were the only people in town that Longarm could say he really knew, and they were busy. Jason had said he would be by after he closed the store and would walk with Longarm to see the kid. It was probably sensible to wait for Jason to walk with him, just in case he lost his balance and needed help. But it was damned boring to sit there with nothing to do and not even any books to pass the time. Longarm finished his cheroot and flicked the stub onto the patch of bare dirt that passed for a front yard.

The barn was at the other end of the street. That was not more than a hundred yards or so. Piece of cake.

Longarm held onto the railing while he carefully negotiated the steps down from the porch, tugged the brim of his Stetson down to a better angle, and set off down the dusty street.

Damn, but a hundred yards could be a mighty long way.

By the time he got to the express company barn, his legs felt as limp as wet rope and he was actually gasping for breath. Incredible that he could have gotten so far out of shape so quickly.

He stopped for a moment at the front of the barn to catch his breath, then stepped into the cool shade inside. The place smelled of bright hay and horse manure. There were three large stalls on each side of a broad center aisle. Four of them were occupied, the horses huge, heavy-bodied draft stock.

Longarm could see inquisitive ears focused in his direction at the sound of his footsteps entering the place, and four dark shapes shifted back and forth.

He bypassed the horses and looked into the last stall on the right. The freckle-faced redhead was there, all right. Chained to the wall with sturdy trace chain and a padlock. The hard steel was looped tight around the boy's neck so there was no possibility he would be able to slip free, as might have been possible if the chain was wrapped around his waist.

The boy stared back at Longarm with more hate than dread. His jaw was clamped hard shut and his expression was coldly defiant. He sat leaning back against the post to which he was chained, knees drawn up and arms wrapped around them. He was barefoot, Longarm saw, and his

14

clothes were ragged and dirty now, but once had been of decent quality.

His huge, china blue eyes locked onto Longarm, but the boy said nothing.

More because his legs were becoming weak than from any desire to be companionable, Longarm too sat on the clean straw that had been tossed into the stall for bedding. He sat down, crossed his legs at the ankles, and leaned back against a side wall of the stall.

"What's your name, boy?"

The kid silently stared.

"D'you remember who I am, boy? D'you recognize me from when you stuck me with your knife?"

Again there was no answer.

"Did anybody think t' tell you who I am?"

The kid's eyes seemed deep enough to walk into. Longarm had to wonder just what the boy had seen in his few years to make him so tough and unyielding.

Unlike their first encounter, this time Longarm had his wallet and badge with him. He pulled the wallet out and flipped it open. "I'm a U.S. deputy marshal, son. Custis Long is my name. Longarm if you like, like in the long arm o' the law. Which you ought to care about seein' as how you've committed an assault on a federal peace officer." He closed the wallet and replaced it inside his coat.

Still the boy said nothing.

"The doc tells me you came within a couple inches o' murdering me, in which case you'd likely hang, never mind your age. Murdering deputy marshals generally ain't a good idea. You're old enough you ought t' know that already. For that matter, murdering anybody ain't a good idea. Other folks frown on it, y'see."

Longarm waited, but the boy said nothing.

He wanted a smoke, but it would not be a good idea to light up inside the barn, particularly one filled with hay and dry straw.

15

He sat like that for ten minutes or more until his legs regained some strength. The red-haired boy's gaze never wavered and the kid did not say a word in that time.

Eventually, with a grunt Longarm stood and brushed the straw off the back of his trousers.

"We got plenty o' time, you an' me," he said, "you because it could be more'n a month till the circuit judge comes through here, me because I still got a lot o' healing t' do from where you cut me. I'll be back tomorrow. We'll talk some more then."

Longarm turned and slowly, very carefully, walked out into the aisle and toward the sunshine at the other end of it.

Chapter 5

At breakfast the next morning, walking was a little easier, a little steadier. Improvement was slow, but he was making progress.

Longarm ate, then speared a couple extra pork chops off the platter and used the side of his fork to scrape the pan gravy off them. He made a beggar's-bindle fold out of his napkin and deposited the chops there, carrying the little bundle with him when he left. If Jonesy, the man who ran the place, noticed, he said nothing. And Longarm did intend to return the napkin later. He was not a thief, after all.

Longarm paused on the boardwalk in front to sit on a bench for a few minutes and smoke a cheroot—he couldn't light up in the barn—then walked down to the express company stable.

The same warm, clean barn scents again greeted him, but this morning there were four different horses in the occupied stalls. The big animals flicked their ears in his direction and one gave a hopeful whicker, but the visitor had nothing for them. He doubted they would have much interest in his pork chops.

"Still here, I see," Longarm said cheerfully when he entered the kid's stall.

The kid jumped and hastily pulled his hands away from his fly. Caught the little SOB pounding his pud? Could be. Longarm sure as hell knew what that tool was for at the boy's age, and none of those old wives' tales about it stunting a boy's growth had turned out to be true. Hadn't turned out to stop him from doing it either.

"Put it away, boy, an' wipe your hands clean. I got something for you." He handed the napkin to the kid. The boy accepted the package despite the hate in his eyes.

When he unfastened the knot at the top and laid the napkin open to expose the pork chops, he glanced up with a sharp look, but he said nothing to his benefactor. Without a word, he grabbed a chop off his lap and began wolfing down the tender meat.

Longarm suspected the boy's diet had consisted mostly of porridge or grits or boiled potatoes ever since he was chained here. A kid can live on that, but there is nothing like a pork chop—especially one with a lot of fat on it—to capture his attention.

"My name is Custis Long. D'you remember that?" Longarm waited a moment, then said, "Still not talking, eh? Your choice, boy."

Longarm again settled cross-legged onto the straw and patiently waited. The boy said nothing and neither did Longarm. After half an hour or so, the pork bones had been polished practically to a shine and Longarm thought he was in grave danger of perishing for lack of a smoke. He stood and said, "You got t' give me them bones an' napkin back, son."

In response to the questioning look in the boy's eyes, he said, "Pork bones can be awful sharp. I've heard of cons in prison rubbing them on stone to make points an' using them for knives. That's why when you get to prison you won't be eating any meat except soft bits in stews an' like that. I'll bring you some more tomorrow."

At the stall door, he paused and looked back. "I'll bring

18

something for you t' eat tomorrow, kid, but if I do you're gonna have t' thank me for it. Right out loud. You understand? You are gonna have t' speak to me if you want me t' do for you."

He had misjudged the depth of the boy's determination and taken it too far. He could see it in the stubborn set of the little bastard's chin and in the sullen defiance that lay inside those unblinking eyes.

"I'll see you tomorrow, kid."

Longarm's hand was reaching for a cheroot before he had taken two steps toward the sunshine and fresh air.

Chapter 6

"Abner, I reckon it's time for me t' be moving along now," Longarm said after lunch three days later. "Jason says my belly can stand up to the bumping an' bouncing o' that coach now, so it's time I get back to work."

"Oh, you can't go now," the stationmaster protested. "We need you to testify against the boy when Judge Randall gets here."

"Otis Randall?"

"You know him?" Sluter asked.

"Oh, I know him, all right. He's a stickler. Won't let nobody get away with nothing."

"Judge Randall is riding circuit this term," Sluter said, "and he will want to question the complaining witness, Longarm. That is you."

"Dammit, Abner, I can't be hanging around here . . . no offense, but . . . I got work t' do."

"And testifying in a court of law is part of that work. You said so yourself. Why, when your coach stopped here, you were on your way back from giving court testimony. Now we need you to do that here. For us."

"Surely Jason can testify as t' what the boy done."

"And just as surely Judge Randall will want to know

why the offended party is not present his own self. We've talked it over, the town council and me, and we all agree that we don't want to let that boy go with scarcely a reprimand. The next person he stabs could well die. It isn't right that he be turned loose."

"Wouldn't exactly be right for a kid that age t' go to prison neither. You know what would happen to him there. A young'un like that . . . Abner, he'd have an asshole the size of Montana practically before the cell door clanged shut."

"We talked about that too, Longarm. We intend to ask the judge to send him to the Home for Boys back in Omaha. They would keep him there and see to his education. Give him a trade. Teach him Christian values. But that can't happen unless he is convicted. We need your testimony in order for that to happen."

"I'd have t' ask my boss about that," Longarm said.

Sluter grinned. "We've already done that."

"What?"

"The town council sent a wire to Marshal Vail asking to keep you here until the judge arrives."

"When the hell did you do a thing like that?"

"Couple days ago."

"An' what did Billy say?"

"We won't know that until the stage arrives."

"What does the stagecoach have t' do with it, Abner? The horses gonna have Billy's answer tattooed on their butts?"

"Something like that."

Longarm raised his eyebrows.

"You may not have noticed it, Mr. Sees-Everything, but we don't actually have a telegraph wire here. Yet. We're hoping to get one soon. In the meantime, we send notes down to Julesburg by way of the stagecoach and get answers back the same way. We're hoping Marshal Vail's response will be coming by way of the northbound that is due in this evening. In the meantime, we would very much

22

appreciate it if you would stay until we hear back from the marshal." The grin returned. "Which, you may have noticed, you have to do anyway since there won't be another southbound come through until tomorrow morning. Even if you wanted to leave, you couldn't until then."

Longarm sighed. "Then I sure as hell hope Jason has a good supply of cheroots laid in."

"That reminds me. Since you are here as an official witness, your food and lodging will be taken care of by the town council. We've already told Jonesy; you won't be charged for your meals at his café any longer. The town will cover that."

"What about whiskey?"

"This is a dry county, Longarm."

"Hell, I know that. Believe me, I figured that out. Not one damn saloon in the whole place."

Abner glanced around, then lowered his voice. "There is an . . . what you might call an alternative."

"Then tell me. It's been better'n a week since I've had a nip an' my gut keeps asking what it done t' be treated so terrible."

Abner leaned forward and began to whisper instructions.

23

Chapter 7

Longarm felt about as conspicuous as a scarecrow in a corn patch, but Abner had been clear that this was the house. It looked awfully damned respectable for a hog ranch. If there were whores here, they probably lifted their little fingers when they handled their teacups. Still, if this was where a man had to go to get a drink . . .

He mounted the steps and crossed the porch, hesitated briefly at the front door with its etched glass panel and hoity-toity door pull. Then he shrugged and mumbling, "What the hell," pulled the rod that activated a doorbell somewhere inside.

A minute or so later, the door was opened by an extraordinarily attractive woman who was dressed as if getting ready for church—this wasn't Sunday, was it?—or for standing up in front of a classroom full of pupils.

"Ma'am." Longarm snatched his hat off.

"How may I help you, sir?" Oh, she was a fine figure of a woman, this one was. Tall. Almost six feet, he judged. And lean. But she looked strong. Like a rawhide whip. Large, startlingly bright eyes of blue gray. Full mouth and high cheekbones. Handsome despite her age, which he guessed to be something in the neighborhood of fifty. This woman was classy. He had to wonder how she came to be running an illegal outfit out here in the middle of absolutely nothing.

Not that it was his place to ask. The lady had the right to some privacy no matter what she did for a living. "I come t' get a drink, ma'am."

"Very well." She pushed the screen door open so Longarm could enter. "Come inside. May I know your name, sir?"

It was a mite strange that she wouldn't have already been told about the visiting marshal. He would have thought at least one of her customers should have mentioned his presence. Still, he did not want to be discourteous. Longarm introduced himself.

"A deputy marshal, you say?"

"Yes, ma'am."

Her eyes dropped toward the big Colt that rode at his waist. "How exciting."

"Yes, ma'am. Uh, about that drink?"

"Yes, of course. Please sit over there, Marshal." She pointed toward a settee in her front room, and Longarm dutifully went to it and rather gingerly lowered himself onto it. With those spindly curved legs, the thing did not look like it could bear the weight of a butterfly, much less a grown man. But it held when he sat on it, perched on the very forward edge lest he fall when the settee collapsed beneath him. He was distinctly uncomfortable. "Now. What is it you would have of me, Marshal?"

"Like I said, ma'am. I'm just wantin' a drink."

"So you did." She gave him a very brief smile. Lordy, she was one fine, handsome woman indeed. Severe and proper, though, one of those women he couldn't imagine dropping her drawers to take a shit like a normal human being. Maybe her turds came out wrapped in perfumed paper. Now wouldn't that be something to see. "Did I say something to amuse you, Marshal?"

26

"No, ma'am. Why d'you ask?"

"Just wondering what brought on that wicked smile just now."

"Smile? Me?" Hadn't realized he had done it. And he damned sure was not going to tell her the cause. Perfumed turds indeed! "Sorry." He clasped his hands tight together and told himself to act proper in front of this lady. "What was you saying now?"

"Your drink," she responded. "You said you came to my door in search of a drink."

"Yes, ma'am, that is it exactly."

"And what sort of drink would you care to have, Marshal Long?"

"Why . . . whiskey, o' course. I been dry for way the hel—for way too long now, an' I didn't happen to be carryin' a bottle in my gear when I got stabbed."

"You were stabbed?" The lady seemed quite shocked. How the hell had she managed to avoid hearing about that much excitement in a settlement this small?

"Yes, ma'am. Stabbed. By that boy over at Bradley's store."

"By a *boy*, you say?"

"Yes, ma'am."

"What boy?"

"Nobody seems t' know whose he is nor where he belongs. He just showed up. Tried t' steal some stuff. When I went t' stop him is when he stabbed me."

"And no one knows who he is?"

"No, ma'am, an' he ain't talking. Not to nobody. Kid is maybe ten or eleven years old but tough as nails. Won't even say his name."

"Dear me. That is quite awful. Where is the boy now?"

"Abner Sluter an' the town council got him sittin' in chains inside a stall over to the express comp'ny barn."

"In chains, you say?"

"Yes, ma'am."

"And so young." She shook her head and softly clucked.

"About that drink, ma'am . . . ," Longarm prompted.

"Yes, of course. Your, um, whiskey." She said that like the word "whiskey" left a bad taste in her mouth. "I do not know whose practical joke sent you to my doorstep, but not a drop of vile alcohol has ever passed my lips. Nor shall it. Ever. I could offer you water, tea, coffee, even lemonade. But not hard spirits. Never spirits."

Longarm leaped to his feet. He could feel his cheeks begin to heat up in blushing embarrassment. "Ma'am, I am so awful sorry, I don't know what the hell t' tell you about this, but it was an honest mistake. Please b'lieve me about that. It was an honest mistake."

"Yes. Perhaps it was." That faint smile flickered again, then quickly faded away. The lady extended her hand and Longarm very lightly touched her fingertips, as he understood was the correct way to shake hands with a proper lady like this.

Apologizing and practically stumbling over himself as he hurried out, he was all the way down the steps and out into the street before he realized that the lady had never introduced herself. He had invaded her home and her privacy, and he had no idea who the hell she was.

Chapter 8

"Keep that up an' you're gonna piss your pants," Longarm growled.

Jason Bradley was clutching his belly in pain and doubled over from laughing so hard.

"It . . . it . . . it'd be worth it. Oh. Oh. I wish I had been there to see it. Oh, to be a fly on the wall. Ah!" Bradley managed to straighten upright as his howling subsided. He wiped his eyes, looked at Longarm, and with a snort started laughing all over again.

"I don't see what's so almighty funny 'bout this," Longarm grumbled.

"Oh, but . . . you actually went inside and asked for a *drink*?"

"Yes, dammit, but I woulda swore I was where Abner said I could get a whiskey."

"Not damned likely. Not from the Widow Hayes."

"Widow lady, is she?"

"Yes, and as far as I know, no one around here has any idea what her first name is. She was married to a man, construction engineer of some sort and apparently pretty well off. They traveled a lot, kept to themselves when they were here between projects. Then one time she came back by

29

herself, well, just her and her maid. The maid said Frank Hayes was killed in some sort of accident. His widow hasn't hardly been outside the walls of that house ever since. And no one from here has been inside. Except you." Bradley began laughing again.

"Shit," Longarm mumbled. "So how'd I get it wrong? Where should I've gone?"

"You turned the wrong way. The hog ranch is completely on the other end of town from the Hayes place."

"But Abner said . . ."

Bradley snorted again. "Abner Sluter is one of the nicest men I know, but the man couldn't find his ass with both hands. He gets directions wrong all the time. Lucky for him the coach drivers already know where to go, and folks around here know better than to ask Abner for directions. Hell, Abner couldn't find his own outhouse without a map." Jason's lip twitched and his eyes watered, and within seconds he was doubled over in a fresh gale of guffaws.

When Bradley's laughter subsided again, he rubbed his face with the heels of both hands and, shaking his head, said, "Give me five minutes to finish sweeping up in here. It's closing time anyway, so I will walk over there with you to show you the way. You can buy me a drink by way of a thank you."

"All right. But dammit all anyhow."

Jason began chuckling all over again.

Chapter 9

Whiskey had never tasted so good, Longarm thought. Even if it was Irish instead of his beloved Maryland-distilled rye. He raised his glass in a silent salute to Jason Bradley, then tossed off the remainder of that first whiskey. "Another," he said to the fat woman who was running the hog ranch. Lucky for him he was required to enforce federal laws, but did not have to care a fig about violations of local regulations. "By all means another for me an' for my friend here."

"Not for me, thanks. I have to get home," Jason said.

Longarm nodded and thanked Bradley again for acting as his guide and local mentor. Jason finished his drink and left. Not wanting to intrude in private conversations, Longarm carried his second whiskey to a small table well away from the group of men standing by the bar. He took out a cheroot and used his pocketknife to carefully trim off the twist, then struck a match and savored the taste of both tobacco and Irish. They seemed a fine combination.

Half an hour or so later, Longarm wandered up the dusty street to the café where he had been taking his meals. "Steak and potatoes for me tonight, Jonesy," he said firmly.

"What I got tonight is stew. Take it or leave it."

"I'll take it, thank you."

"If it makes you feel any better, the stew has taters in it. Meat too, but you'll be happier if you don't ask what kind."

"Oh, that really makes me feel *much* better," Longarm said with a grin.

"One bowl of sardine stew coming up," the café owner said.

"You aren't . . ."

It was Jonesy's turn to grin. "No, I ain't serious. But I had you for a minute there."

It was a good thing that folks were beginning to josh around with him, Longarm knew. It meant he was being accepted into their community despite his badge.

By the time Longarm was done with his meal—the meat was most likely antelope—it was fully dark outside. Longarm paused on the street to light a cheroot. He considered whether he should go back to the express company stables and take another stab at talking to the boy. But dammit, this was too pleasant an evening to let it be ruined by a sullen kid like that, he decided. Tomorrow would be time enough.

On the other hand, the prospect of turning in at such an early hour was not particularly appealing either. Perhaps he could find a friendly card game back at that hog ranch.

As he approached the place, he heard scuffling and several low grunts coming from behind a row of stunted bushes in the side yard. Longarm veered away from the path that led up to the front porch, and headed into the shadows on the far side of the house.

There were three dark figures there, dimly visible in the light that seeped down from the stars and a cloudless sky. Two large figures and one very small one. The small one seemed to be wearing a dress. But not for long if the larger figures had their way about it. Those two looked to be intent on ripping the clothes off the small woman who struggled between them.

The two picked the woman up between them and flung her down to the ground. Hard.

One pinned her wrists to the earth while the other flipped her dress up and tried to pry her legs apart.

The woman struggled in silence except for some grunts of effort, kicking and turning and making things difficult for the man who wanted to rape her.

Difficult. But not impossible. If the two men kept at her, they would get what they wanted despite the little woman's efforts.

Unless somebody intervened.

Longarm tossed his cheroot down and stepped into the shadows with them.

He gauged the distance carefully. Smiled. And before any of them knew he was there, kicked one of the attackers in the nuts.

That one howled and fell forward on top of the woman, clutching himself like he thought he was ruined. Could be that he was, but Longarm was not concerned about that.

The other man yelped and stood upright just in time for Longarm's fist to turn his nose into pulp. Blood, black in the starlight, began to flow. "Hey," the man protested. "We was just having us a little fun." He was holding a cloth to his face, trying to stanch the flow of blood but not doing a very good job of it. His voice was thick and nasal.

"Looked t' me like the lady wasn't having as much fun as you boys was," Longarm said.

"She ain't no lady. She's a nigger."

"Just a nigger whore," the other one put in as, still holding his crotch, he tried to crawl onto his feet.

"Mister, I don't care who nor what she is. If the *lady*"—he emphasized the word—"says no, then you damn well better leave be. Or d'you want me t' haul your asses down to Julesburg an' file charges agin you?" That much was pure bluff. Julesburg was not even in the same state as this little hamlet, and as a federal officer Longarm had no jurisdiction over local matters anyway.

The one whose balls Longarm had crushed managed to

drag himself upright. He weaved and wobbled some, but he was standing. "We didn't mean nothing. Just wanted a little piece of ass."

"Yeah. Without paying for it," Longarm said.

"We woulda paid," the one with the broken nose mumbled.

"And pigs would of flew too," Longarm said. "Both of you, get out of my sight before I decide t' put you in cuffs an' take you in." The truth was that in his "sight" was something of an overstatement. In the darkness, he still had not gotten a good enough look at either of them to be sure he would recognize them the next time he saw them.

Well, he thought with a grin, maybe the fellow with the busted nose. He likely would recognize that one by the twin black eyes he would be sporting for a spell, even after the swelling went down in that snout. He'd be looking like a raccoon for the next week or more.

As for the other one, he ought to be able to straighten up and walk properly by tomorrow sometime.

"Get outa here," Longarm snarled.

They did.

Longarm removed his hat and gave a little half bow toward the woman, who was now sitting up and had pushed her skirts down where they belonged. "Are you all right, miss? Here. Let me help you up." He extended his hand, and felt her very small hand slip trustingly into his.

34

Chapter 10

"Sorry 'bout those two, ma'am. I reckon they were drunk."

"It is all right, sir. Thank you for helping me."

"My pleasure, ma'am. Are you all right? No harm to you, I trust."

"It is 'miss' actually. My name is Jennie Williard. And I . . . I am no stranger to assaults and abuse. But no, I suffered no harm this time. I don't believe I know you, sir."

Longarm smiled. "Save your 'sirs' for my boss. I don't rate that high. My name is Custis Long."

"Oh, yes. You are the gentleman who visited Miz Hayes earlier."

He laughed. "Visited. That's a nice way t' put it. But Lordy, has everybody in this town heard 'bout that already?"

"I heard it straight from the horse's mouth, so to speak. But don't you dare tell Miz Hayes I said that."

"Not that I expect to see the lady again now that I know she isn't selling whiskey there. I wouldn't have no reason t' tell her even if I was t' set in her parlor again. So how'd you come t' hear about my mistake, Miss Jennie Williard?"

"You see, I work for Miz Hayes. I'm her maid."

Longarm glanced toward the hog ranch, where liquor most definitely *was* available.

"There's some, well, some girls, you should understand," Jennie very haltingly said. "Girls who, you know, do things."

"I understand."

"One of them is a colored girl. Like me. Her and me, we're the only coloreds for miles and miles around. We get together sometimes to set and drink coffee together. Just, you know, being with our own kind, I suppose you would say."

"I can understand that," Longarm said.

"This evening I gave Miz Hayes her supper. Then I came over here to visit with Lucretia. She doesn't start work till after supper time, and I'm free to do whatever I want after supper. That don't give us much time to visit, but it's a pleasure when we do."

"Then I should get out of your way and let you enjoy your visit," Longarm said.

"Oh, we were done. Miz Helen called her girls to the parlor to get ready for the gentlemen guests. Lucretia and me was done visiting. I was on my way home when . . . you know . . . when those two gentlemen grabbed me."

"Huh. Those two weren't gentlemen, believe me."

"Oh, sir, I learned a whole long time ago that for me every white gentleman is a gentleman whether he really is one or not."

"Smart girl," Longarm said. "It's just a shame you have t' feel that way."

"Now if you'll excuse me, sir, I'd best be getting home so's you can go in and have your fun. But if you want a good girl, clean and nice, you pick that colored girl and tell her that her friend Jennie says she should be real nice to you."

"I came here lookin' for a drink, not a girl," Longarm said, "but I thank you for that advice. You're going home now?"

"Yes, sir."

"Then let me walk with you. I want to see you safely

36

there. Just in case those two drunks have ideas about jump-
ing you again."

"You don't have to do that, sir."

"I want to. And stop calling me 'sir.' "

"Yes, sir."

Longarm began to laugh, and after a moment Jennie did
as well.

"D'you live with Miz Hayes?"

"Yes, sir. Kind of. She don't keep no horse or buggy so
she gave me the little barn out back of her house to live in.
I cleaned it out and fixed it up real nice. Like a real house
almost. I'll show you if you like."

"Yes, Jennie, I'd like that. Now. May I walk you home?"

"Yes, sir."

"Stop calling me s—"

"Yes, si . . . yes, Mr. Long."

"My friends call me Longarm," he suggested. "Try that
instead."

"Yes, sir. I mean . . . well . . ."

"Don't worry about it. Say whatever is comfortable for
you. Now come on. Let me walk you home." He offered his
arm and squired her away down the main street for anyone
to see who wanted to look.

Chapter 11

Jennie's little stable was more dollhouse than shack. Originally, the place had been intended to house a horse and, in a bay beside the horse stall, a small buggy or carriage. Jennie obviously had spent a great amount of time and effort to turn it into a home.

The horse stall was now her bedroom and the carriage bay her parlor and reading room. A small sheepherder's stove, an armoire, and some shelving had been installed in the tiny runway that fronted the stall and the bay. A low fire chuckled pleasantly in the little stove now, the warmth from it feeling nice after the cool night air outside.

The walls were covered with muslin fabric—probably cast-off curtains from some finer dwelling—and the furniture was a mixture of other people's leavings that Jennie had brought together in a surprisingly comfortable whole.

Longarm removed his hat and remarked on how nice everything looked.

"Thank you, sir. I . . . I don't have any whiskey to offer you, but I put some water on to heat before I went off to visit with Lucretia. It should be hot now if you'd like some tea."

Longarm detested tea. He would rather drink dishwater. "I'd love a cup o' tea, miss."

"It will take only a few minutes for the tea to steep. Sit over there. Please." She pointed to an armchair with deep upholstery and a mismatched footstool, obviously her own favorite reading area as it was flanked by lamp stands and a book lay close to hand on the floor.

Jennie turned the wicks higher on the two lamps she had left burning, and went around the walls lighting more until the place was cozily bright and homey.

She returned and perched on an upholstered stool, and for the first time Longarm was able to get a good look at Mrs. Hayes's Negro maid.

The girl's color was light chocolate. Her skin was smooth and creamy. Her hair was short, tight ringlets contained beneath a mob cap. She was a little bit of a thing, probably not five feet tall, and he doubted she could make a hundred pounds if she carried a five-pound barbell in each hand. Pale eyes and thin lips suggested a good amount of white blood somewhere in her family tree. She was, he thought, quite pretty.

"You are the first gentleman ever to visit me."

"Here, you mean?" He motioned with his hand to indicate this stable that she had turned into a home for herself.

"Oh, no, sir, I meant anywheres. I've never had a gentleman to tea. Or anything else." She dropped her eyes. "I've known a lot like those two over by the whorehouse, but never a real gentleman such as yourself."

"Why, Jennie, I'm real proud t' be your first admirer. First among many yet to come, I would suspect."

"Do you mean that, sir? The 'admirer' part, I mean?"

Longarm nodded. "I surely do. You are a very pretty girl, Jennie Williard." He meant that too even if he was still trying to figure out her age. With that smooth, perfect skin and huge eyes—and with Longarm's lack of experience with Negro women—she could be anywhere from twenty to fifty or beyond. Whatever she was, she was damned attractive, and he told her so.

"You're mighty nice, sir. Could I ask you for a favor? A real big favor?"

"Of course. I won't make any promises until I hear what it is that you want, but I'll be glad t' listen."

"Could you . . . sir, I've never known such a nice man as you. And I've never in my life been held by a gentleman that wasn't trying to tear my clothes off and rape me. Would you . . . would you be willing to hold me? Just for a minute is all I'm asking. I'm clean. I washed all over before I went to see Lucretia. And I . . ."

"Hush talking," Longarm gently said, holding his arms out and motioning for the girl to come onto his lap. "Come set here an' let me hold an' cuddle you."

Chapter 12

She was soft and small and very shy. He thought she had fallen asleep with her face pressed to his neck beneath his chin, but she was merely being quiet. After a while, he felt very lightly the touch of her lips. And then of her tongue.

"You taste nice," she murmured, so faintly he could scarcely hear. A little later she whispered, "I feel safe with you."

Longarm smiled. "I hope you always will be, Jennie. Always."

"Would you do me another big, big favor, sir?"

"Maybe. If you'll stop calling me sir . . ." Then he shut up. Her giggling made him realize that this time her use of the word had been intentional rather than a slip of the tongue.

"Would you be willing to make love to a colored girl?"

"Depends on the girl, Jennie. I have in the past. An' some I haven't wanted to." He smiled and gently rocked her, holding her tight on his lap where she could almost certainly feel his body's reaction to her presence. His pecker was standing tall, and so hard it would take a chisel to make a dent in it.

"Would you . . . with me?"

"With you, Jennie, I would be honored."

"The buttons on this dress is in the back in case you haven't noticed," she whispered.

The girl's chest was as flat as a boy's, but with long, puffy nipples that were as dark as little lumps of coal standing out from a chocolate plain. He could feel each rib and the contours of her spine as he ran his hands over her tiny body.

Jennie moaned softly when he began to lick and suckle at her nipples.

"That feels . . . oh, that feels so good. So good. I didn't know."

He licked his way north, running his tongue over her dark, smooth flesh until he reached her neck.

Longarm picked the girl up, cradling her in his arms when he stood. He paused there to kiss her, his tongue probing between her lips. She tasted faintly of mint, he thought. A cup of mint tea shared with her friend? Quite likely.

Jennie laid her head trustingly against his shoulder as he carried her around the shoulder-high partition that separated the carriage bay from what once had been a horse stall.

Her bed was narrow, built only for one. But it would accommodate two if the two needed only space enough for one. He placed her on the bed and held a finger to her lips, then stepped back a pace so he could admire the girl's naked body.

Her belly was flat and her hip bones sharp, her waist impossibly small. There seemed hardly an ounce of meat anywhere on her. Her pubic hair was jet black and tightly curly. A sheen of moisture glistened on the bright red lips of her pussy.

Longarm shed his clothes quickly and joined her on the bed, kneeling between her wide-spread thighs. He lowered himself over her and kissed her again, his tongue probing into her mouth, but this time encountering her own inquisitive tongue trying to investigate him.

Jennie sighed and smiled, then tugged at his waist, urging him down. Urging him into her.

The blind snake found its way, bumping into her wet and dripping pussy lips, then sliding slow and deep inside her flesh.

Moist heat surrounded and soothed him. He filled her body with his and stayed there for a while, poised and motionless, enjoying the feel of her engulfing him.

It was Jennie who began to move first, pumping her hips ever so lightly up and down, her belly nudging his with each increasingly rapid thrust.

Jennie's breath became ragged and she gasped for air. But she did not slow the furious pace of her lovemaking.

Longarm held her tight and speared her with his living lance until she cried out and went into a spasm of delight. That was enough to send him over the edge too and he thrust powerfully, deep inside her, as his seed spurted from his body into hers. It flowed in a hot, sweet gush, and Jennie hungrily milked him of everything he had to offer.

"Thank you," she said when Longarm finally, slowly, withdrew. Then her face twisted into an impish grin and she added, "Sir."

Longarm laughed. And kissed her.

Chapter 13

It was late when he finally left Jennie Williard's little love nest behind the Hayes house. Longarm stood for a moment, just enjoying the freshness of the cool evening breeze. A moment was long enough, though. Cool began to feel more like cold, and he found himself wanting both a drink and a cigar before he turned in for the night.

He lit a cheroot—he needed to buy more come morning when the mercantile opened for business again—and commenced hiking.

The walk across town was enough to warm him up a little. There was still a light showing inside the hog ranch. Thank goodness. He was afraid the place might have closed for the night already, folks in farming country going generally early to bed.

"Evenin', Helen," he said to the fat woman who ran the place. "I'll take a mug o' that good Irish, if you please."

"Lay your money down then."

"The town is taking care of my needs while I'm here," Longarm said. Not that he really expected the town council to cover his drinking as well as his meals and lodging. But what the hell. It was worth a try.

"Says you. But I got to give you credit. You at least

47

come up with a new excuse for not paying, and here I thought I'd already heard 'em all."

Longarm laid a coin down, and the woman grunted with satisfaction, then reached for the bottle.

The whiskey tasted as good as he remembered. While he drank it, he glanced over the tiny flock of doves gathered in a back corner waiting for customers, most of whom seemed to have deserted them at this hour.

It was obvious which of the painted and powdered girls was Jennie's friend Lucretia. She was a tall, angular black girl. The others suggested that Helen for some reason preferred darker flesh in her working staff. Three of the girls appeared to be Indians and one was likely Mexican. Perhaps they came cheaper, Longarm thought, and were easier managed.

Not that he had any interest in any of them. Jennie had more than taken care of his needs for the time being, and she had made it plain that she would welcome return visits for as long as he was around.

Which, he hoped, would not be all that long. Hopefully, Billy Vail would put a word in Judge Randall's ear about releasing him so he could get back to doing his duty. In the meantime, between this Irish whiskey and Jennie Williard, things were not all bad.

Longarm finished his whiskey and set the mug down. He was just turning toward the door when two men walked in. Longarm began to smile just a little.

Seemed that he knew these boys. Not that he had ever properly met them before, but he had certainly seen them. And more.

The taller and heavier of the two walked carefully. As if perhaps he had a deep and lingering ache somewhere just south of his belly. His pal had a pair of shiners and dried blood on his shirt.

"There's the son of a bitch," the taller one snarled. "Get him."

48

"Don't even think about it," Longarm warned. "I put you down once. If I have t' do it again, you ain't gonna be happy afterward."

"You snuck up on us before. That won't happen again."

"We're gonna break you apart, mister."

"It ain't 'mister.' It's 'deputy,' an' I'm a deputy United States marshal so don't fuck with me."

"Your badge don't mean shit to us, mister."

"What're you gonna do? Take it out and hit us with it?"

"Think you can kick me in the balls and get away with it, mister?"

"Oh, I think I already did that."

"Except the fight you started ain't over yet, mister."

"Have it your way," Longarm said.

"We ain't carrying guns, mister."

The sensible thing would be to remind these brutes that while they might not be carrying guns, he was. And would use his guns if they pushed him.

But dammit, he just plain did not like the sort of man who would assault a girl and take her against her will. The way he saw it every girl, even those whores over there in the corner, had a right to tell a man no, and the kind of low sonuvabitch who would commit rape was badly in need of a lesson.

These two quite obviously had not learned their lesson.

Longarm removed his tweed coat, carefully folded it, and laid it on the bar beside his empty mug. He unbuckled his gunbelt and laid it on top of the coat.

When he turned toward the door, the two men were grinning. They separated, one sidling left and the other right. Longarm had the impression that this was a hunting tactic they had used before.

He grinned right back at them. If these bastards wanted to play, then he was their boy.

"Loser pays for any damages," Helen warned from behind the bar.

Not that there was anything of value in the place, Long-arm thought. It was the sort of joint that would be torn apart at least a couple times a week. And likely the fat woman would collect damage payments each time.

And on top of that . . . he did not damn well intend to be the loser who would be shaken down for damage repayment.

He wheeled to his right and charged straight at the gent with the raccoon eyes.

Chapter 14

Coon Eyes flinched and tried to duck out of the way, but he was not Longarm's target. Yet

Longarm figured—correctly as it turned out—that whichever one he went for, the other one would try to come in behind and jump him.

As soon as Coon Eyes started to turn away, Longarm pivoted and lashed out at Broken Nuts, who was coming hard toward what he expected to be Longarm's blind side.

Longarm's fist met him flush on the nose. Flesh pulped and blood flew, and in another hour or so Broken Nuts should have a pair of black eyes that would nicely match the shiners Coon Eyes had already developed.

The man bellowed like an enraged bull. He shook his head, slinging blood in both directions, then came on again, growling out loud and making a show of being menacing. There had to be a reason for that, Longarm figured.

Longarm heard a rush of movement behind him and quickly ducked, spinning away from Coon Eyes, who had already launched a wild swing that would damn near have taken Longarm's head off had it landed. Instead, it swept past, glancing off the top of Longarm's shoulder. The force of the blow was so strong it pulled Coon Eyes halfway around.

Never one to overlook a gift horse, Longarm took the opportunity to tattoo Coon Eyes with a quick left-right combination over the man's left kidney, then spun again to face Broken Nuts.

That gentleman was escalating things. He had snatched up a heavy brass spittoon and was preparing to brain Longarm with it.

"I don't think so," Longarm muttered. He grabbed Broken Nuts by the wrist with his left hand and threw a hard underhand punch to the pit of the man's belly with his right.

While that was occupying the man's interest, Longarm twisted with his left hand. Hard. The cuspidor rotated in the fellow's grip and, water flowing downhill as it most generally does, the contents of the spittoon flowed out. Gushed out actually. All over Broken Nuts.

Phlegm. Tobacco juice. Cigar butts. Pipe dottle. Just plain old spit. The accumulation of however long it had been since anyone got around to cleaning the spittoons. All were there in a slimy, stinking mess. All poured out onto the shoulder and chest of Broken Nuts. The man turned pale and dropped to his knees, commencing to retch even before he hit the floor, the contents of his latest meal going there ahead of him.

Longarm did not take time to savor that small victory. He wheeled quickly again to face Coon Eyes in time to see that one pick up a chair to hit him with.

"Oh, shit," the man groaned when he saw Longarm come at him.

"Too late," Longarm said. He took hold of the chair and pushed, shoving Coon Eyes back across the floor step by step until his back was pressed hard against the wall.

"We didn't . . . we wasn't going to . . ."

"Shut your hole, shithead. I ain't listening." Longarm

wrenched the chair out of the man's grasp and flung it aside. Coon Eyes dropped to his knees and began blubbering.

"Don't hurt me, mister, for God's sake don't hurt me."

Longarm grunted and turned away, satisfied to end the scrape there. He hadn't taken more than three steps toward the bar to reclaim his coat and gunbelt when he heard a whisper of movement and saw the fat bar woman's eyes go wide.

He spun back around again in time to see Coon Eyes coming up from the floor fast, a knife in his fist.

"Wrong move, asshole," Longarm snarled.

He kicked the knife out of the man's hand. Knelt down and extended the suddenly unresisting man's right arm over his knee with his palm upward.

With one quick, powerful shove, Longarm broke the would-be backstabber's elbow.

Coon Eyes shrieked and passed out.

Longarm stood, letting the unconscious man fall to the floor.

Helen's eyes were still wide and staring, but for a different reason now.

"Do I owe you anything for damages?" Longarm asked. Not that there were any. The place was a mess, but nothing significant seemed to have been broken in the melee.

"No. They'll pay if there are any." The fat woman scowled. "Believe me. I'll see to that."

Longarm grinned. "I can believe you 'bout that." He buckled his gunbelt back where it belonged, pulled the big Colt out of the leather, and flipped the loading gate open so he could check the cartridges—after all, the weapon had been out of his possession for a little while there—then put his hat and coat back on. "Thanks for the hospitality, ma'am," he said, and politely touched the brim of his Stetson before walking out into the night. It was late and he was ready for some sleep now.

Chapter 15

"I can't believe you folks don't have the telegraph up here yet," Longarm grumbled the next morning when he handed Abner Sluter the message he wanted sent to Billy Vail. The note would have to be carried by hand down to Julesburg and sent from there.

Abner shrugged. "In due time, I suppose. The fellow who was supposed to string wire went bankrupt and everything . . . wire stock, timber, wagons, right-of-way, all of it is subject to a bunch of suits and countersuits. That wouldn't be so bad except for the right-of-way. Nothing will get straightened out until that is settled, and until then we just have to get along without."

"Fine, but that don't mean I have t' like it." Longarm reached for a cheroot—his last as it turned out—and said, "Are you *sure* there wasn't no message for me with the northbound yesterday evenin'?"

"It will get here when it gets here, Custis, so relax."

"Easy for you t' say."

Abner only shrugged and went out the back door. Longarm left by way of the front. He wanted to go out to the barn where the boy was chained, but he figured there was no great rush about that. He was stuck here for the time being and so was the kid. And right now he intended to go buy some more cheroots while he thought about it. The prospect of being caught out without anything to smoke was ugly. He could get along without tobacco if he had to. But he damn sure would not like it.

Longarm walked over to Jason Bradley's store, and stood off to one side while Jason waited on a lady in a green plaid dress. He got his fistful of cheroots, then waited while Jason silently pondered something. After a moment, Longarm realized what the problem was and said, "It's all right, Jason. The town don't hafta pay for my smokes too. I can handle those my own self."

The shopkeeper looked relieved. He smiled and said, "In that case, you owe me four cents."

Longarm dug in his pockets for a dime, collected his change, and ambled toward the door. He encountered Abner, who was on his way into the store. The express agent was fuming.

"That was quick," Longarm said. "Anything wrong?"

"I'll say there is. I want to have a town council meeting. I think we should administer some sort of justice to that little son of a bitch over there. Do you know what he just did? He spat at me. Look. Right there on my pants leg. See that dark spot? It's spit. The little bastard spat on me."

"You could always turn him loose," Longarm said. "Put him under bond and catch him again later when you're ready to try him."

"Never. I hope the little shit spends the next twenty years in prison."

"For spitting on you?"

"For trying to kill you," Abner snapped. He turned and said, "What do you think, Jason? Can we do anything about that boy?"

"We could release him into Longarm's custody. After all, it was a federal deputy he stuck that knife into. Longarm can have him if he wants the kid."

"That'll be the damn day." Longarm jammed a fresh cheroot between his teeth and headed for the café. Coffee with whoever was there sounded much better than talking to that blank wall of a kid.

He did walk around to the express company barn after lunch, though. Nothing had changed there but the horses. The boy still sat sullenly in the corner of his stall. He gave Longarm one brief, defiant glance and went back to feeling sorry for himself. Or whatever it was he was thinking, alone and miserable like he was.

"It might go easier on you if you'd talk t' me," Longarm said, his voice as gentle as he knew how to make it. "Just tell me why you done what you done, boy. At the very least tell me your name so's we'll know what to write in your prison records."

He might as well have been talking to one of the stage-coach horses.

Longarm stood there for a while, waiting. The boy said nothing. Not that Longarm really expected him to. After a while Longarm turned and left the kid to his private miseries.

Chapter 16

The food at Jonesy's café was becoming tiresome, but Longarm didn't see that he had much choice about it. It was the only place in town where a man could buy a decent meal. Helen over at the hog ranch might have been able to scrape up some jerky and hardtack, but that hardly seemed an improvement over Jonesy's stews. Besides, Longarm was not sure how welcome he would be there after busting up the place earlier. Better to wait a day or two before he showed his face at the unofficial and highly illegal saloon again.

He certainly did not want to go to sleep at this early hour. The sun was barely down and he was a long way from having done anything during the day to tire him out.

Going to bed, on the other hand . . .

Longarm walked out to the edge of town and around behind the Widow Hayes's handsome home.

There was no light showing inside Jennie's place. Likely, she would still be over at the house finishing up her duties for the lady of the manor. Longarm lifted the latch—it was not locked—and let himself in.

He extracted a match from his vest pocket and snapped it aflame with his thumbnail. The match gave light long enough to guide him to Jennie's reading chair.

Longarm laid the spent match carefully onto the low side table where he could find it again to dispose of later, then stretched his legs out and crossed them at the ankles. He tipped his Stetson over his eyes and settled in to wait until the delightful little black girl returned home for the evening.

The way it was supposed to work, Jennie would come home after work. Remove her wrap. Light a lamp. See Longarm sitting there. They would hug and kiss and have a fine old time.

That was the way it was *supposed* to happen.

Except Jennie was not clued in on the "supposed to" part.

What did happen was that Longarm drifted off to sleep in the girl's easy chair. When Jennie came home, she draped her shawl over the partition that separated her sleeping space from the rest of the cabin, then walked in the dark to her chair.

She sat down. On top of a sleeping man.

Startled the shit out of both of them.

Jennie shrieked and jumped like she had been gouged with a cattle prod.

Longarm, equally startled, tried to jump to his feet.

Which spilled Jennie rather rudely off his lap and onto the floor.

He tripped over her. Fell. Fell smack on top of Jennie.

She screamed.

He pulled his Colt and tried to get up. At the same time Jennie was trying to scramble to her feet and get the hell away.

The two of them tangled and fell again.

Longarm, fully awake now, figured it out and hollered, "Hey, hey, it's me, Jen. Don't be scared. It's just me. Custis, I mean."

"Longarm? You . . . you . . . I didn't know you was here."

"I let myself in. Must've fell asleep. I'm sorry."

The girl began to giggle. "I sat right on you."

"Damn sure woke me up too," he said.

Her giggles were contagious, and soon both of them were laughing.

Longarm took her into his arms and kissed her. "There, that's better."

The laughter subsided, replaced by probing tongues and roaming hands. After a moment, Longarm climbed to his feet and helped Jennie up.

"Light me a lamp, pretty girl," he said. "I want t' see you when I take your clothes off an' carry you to the bed."

"Bed? What makes you think you can take me to bed?"

"This." He guided her hand south of his belt buckle and placed it on the bulge in his britches.

She squeezed, then said, "Let go of me so's I can go light that lamp." She giggled again and added, "Sir."

Chapter 17

"Sir."

It was two days later and Longarm was seated at a table in Jonesy's café, enjoying a cup of coffee with a pair of cowboys named Roy and Harry. The two of them were engaged in a game of checkers, and Longarm had been invited to play the winner of their game.

He was a little surprised to see Jennie in town during the day, particularly in the café since she always took her meals in Mrs. Hayes's kitchen.

He was even more surprised when he stood and tried to embrace her. The girl stepped back away from him and dropped into a curtsy. "Sir," she repeated, "Mrs. Eleanor Hayes requests the pleasure of your company at tea this afternoon. Promptly at three if you please, sir. May I tell Mrs. Hayes that you will be joining her?" Jennie curtsied again and stood with her head down and her hands folded in front of her. Very stiff. Very formal. Entirely correct.

He still wanted to hug her, but obviously she did not want the nearly all-white population of the community to think she was overstepping the bounds of propriety. Black girls simply did not have romantic liaisons with white gentlemen. At least not during daylight hours. Longarm stifled his impulses and nodded, just as stiff and proper as Jennie was being.

"Three o'clock? Please tell Mrs. Hayes that I'll be pleased t' call on her then."

"Yes, sir. Thank you, sir."

Longarm thought he saw a hint of a twinkle in the girl's eyes when she curtsied once more, then backed away two steps before turning and leaving the café.

"Well, I'll be a sonuvabitch," Roy said, taking his hand off one of his red checkers and looking up at Longarm.

"Yeah. Ain't that something now. Tea. At three o'clock. Roy, you touched that piece. You got to move it now or lose it. That's the rule, y'know."

"Oh, shit," Roy grumbled.

Longarm pushed his coffee cup away. "Excuse me, fellas. Reckon I'd best go change my shirt an' give my hair a brushing before time for tea." He winked and laughed. Really, though. Who the hell would have thought it?

If nothing else, he thought, at least now he knew what the Widow Hayes's first name was. He had not thought to ask Jennie about that during their nocturnal visits. But then he had been preoccupied with other concerns at those moments.

Three o'clock. Tea. Be damned indeed.

Brushed, buttoned, and carefully inspected by Abner before he walked over, Longarm presented himself at the door to the Hayes house promptly at three. Jennie opened the door to his knock. She curtsied again and stepped aside for him to enter. Once the front door was closed, however, Jennie glanced over her shoulder to make sure her mistress could not see, then came onto tiptoes to kiss Longarm's throat—that was as high as she could reach, even on tiptoes—and give him a brief hug.

"That's better," he said. "For a little while there I thought you was mad at me."

64

"Never," she whispered. In a louder voice, she said, "Come this way please, sir. Mrs. Hayes is in the parlor."

Longarm allowed himself to be announced, then accepted a seat in the chair indicated. Mrs. Hayes was already seated, looking quite elegant in an ivory-colored gown. A small table with sterling silver service on it was laid ready, complete with bone china cups and a teapot hidden beneath a quilted and padded cozy. A plate of finger sandwiches—watercress, he thought—was laid ready as well.

"Thank you for coming, Marshal Long. Would you care for some tea? Or a bite to eat?"

"What I'd most care for, ma'am, is an explanation. I gather this sort o' thing ain't normal. So why'd you ask me in today?"

"You do come right to the point, don't you." She poured tea into one of the cups and handed it to him, then poured another for herself. "There is something I need to discuss with you."

"That's why I'm here, ma'am."

"It is about Petey, marshal."

"I don't know who you mean, ma'am."

"Peter Sanderson."

Longarm shook his head. "Sorry. I don't think I know no Pete Sanderson."

"The *boy*!" she said, exasperated. "The little boy you are keeping in chains out in that awful barn. Surely you have not forgotten him so easily."

"Peter Sanderson? How is it that you know his name, ma'am, an' nobody else in town does?"

"Why, because I asked him, of course."

"Ma'am?"

"Since you mentioned him to me the other day, I became curious. I do have a way with children, if I do say so, and I thought he might feel comfortable speaking with a woman while a man might only intimidate him. I was right

65

about that. Petey is frightened half to death. He needs help. His family needs help. I want you to set him free so he can do what has to be done."

"Ma'am, I got no idea in hell what you're talkin' about."

"Petey, Marshal Long. And his family. His father was murdered, and his mother and sister were kidnapped. Petey is trying to find them and release them."

"The little bastard stuck a knife into me, ma'am. I caught him stealing an' he stuck me. I could show you the scar if you want t' see it."

"Don't be absurd. The child was caught taking some food. He was hungry. He wanted food so he could travel. He wanted to find his mother and his sister. He wants to help them. And he is afraid. Oh, Marshal, that child is so desperately afraid."

"He actually talked t' you, did he?"

"He talks to me, yes. And he has cried with me. You know him as a defiant little criminal, but I have come to see him as just a terrified child with no family and no friends. Let him go, Marshal. Please. Let the child go."

Longarm was so unnerved that he actually took a swallow of the tea before he realized what he was doing and put the cup down.

Chapter 18

"Peter," Mrs. Hayes said, "this is my good friend United States Marshal Custis Long. Marshal, this is my newest friend, Peter Sanderson." The lady smiled and gestured back and forth between them.

The boy was still in chains, but Longarm could see that he had been washed and was wearing a clean shirt for the occasion—obviously the work of Eleanor Hayes.

"Peter, what is it that you have to say to the marshal?"

The kid looked up. Mrs. Hayes was right about one thing. Now that the stubborn defiance was missing from his expression, he looked scared half to death.

"I'm . . . sorry."

"What?" the lady prompted.

"I'm sorry, *sir*."

"That is better, Petey. Thank you. Now tell the marshal how you came to be here."

It was a long story. And not a nice one.

"You heard me right, Abner," Longarm said to the few gentlemen—the town council, more or less—who at Longarm's request were gathered in the McCormick Express

Company office. "I want you t' unchain that boy an' set him free."

"You cannot be serious about that, Marshal," the barber, Kent Weir, said. "He tried to kill you."

"That was a . . . what you call a misunderstandin', Mr. Weir. Besides, as the allegedly aggrieved party, I'm tellin' you that I won't press any charges against him. Fact is, I'm needin' his help to go an' solve a crime."

"He committed *another* crime before he tried to kill you?" Jason grumbled. "Precocious little brat, isn't he."

"You don't understand. None of us did," Longarm said.

"Well, I for one certainly don't understand," Abner said. "Can you please tell us?"

Longarm took out a cheroot and lighted it, then uncrossed his legs and leaned forward. "Peter . . . that's his name, by the way, Peter Sanderson . . . was traveling west with his family. Mother, father, sister, an' him. They couldn't afford the fees to join a train so they was traveling alone, just their one wagon an' team.

"Somewhere south o' here, they was joined one evening by four men who asked could they share the fire an' their food. Except they brought whiskey instead o' food. They ate what Miz Sanderson cooked, an' I guess they made some pretty lewd remarks about Miz Sanderson, who was doin' the cooking, an' Betty Sanderson, who was serving it to them.

"The more they drank, the nastier they got. The boy didn't understand what-all the men was sayin', but I think the picture is pretty clear. They was commencing to get downright rank.

"The upshot of it all was that Petey's pa told the men t' leave his camp. Them, they didn't bat an eye, the way Petey tells it. They hauled out their hoglegs and shot Mr. Sanderson down, then grabbed hold of Miz Sanderson and the girl . . . Betty is sixteen and Petey doesn't see it, but

68

others say the girl is awful pretty . . . and tried to nab Petey too, but he turned rabbit and bolted.

"It was night and he ran like hell t' get away. Which he did, but in the process he got himself lost. He eventually found his way back to his family's wagon. What was left of it. He said the wagon had been looted an' then burned. The horses, along with his ma and his sister, were gone. He didn't have no food, no gun, no nothing, but he was determined he was gonna go after those four men. Just him alone. That's what he was doin' here—tryin' to steal food so's he could travel.

"What he expected t' do once he caught up with the men . . . he hadn't worked that out yet. An' he was distrustful of us . . . you an' me an' all of us . . . because we was men an' it was men that stole his family."

"What about his father?" Jason asked.

"Petey said his pa was killed outright. Said he scraped up a bit of a mound to lay his father under. Said he didn't know what he could do past that an' didn't know the words that should be said, so that's all he done. Said there's no marker or anything, just a patch of bare dirt somewhere on the prairie."

"That's an interesting yarn."

"If it's true."

"Gentlemen," Longarm said, "I got no reason to think it ain't true. Sounds to me like there's a woman an' a girl bein' held in involuntary servitude." He smiled. "An' that goes against the laws of these here United States, which means I got the authority . . . in fact the *duty* . . . to pursue them criminals an' see this to a conclusion.

"That bein' the case, gents, come tomorra morning I figure t' borrow two saddle horses an' take after them. I'll be takin' the boy along as a guide an' to identify the kidnappers once I catch up to them. Oh, an' Jason, when I came away from Denver I was just expectin' to sit through a trial.

I didn't bring my Winchester along. Reckon I'll be obliged to ask for the borrow of one off you."

"What about? . . ."

Longarm held a hand up. "The United States gummint will pay for the hire o' the horses an' for any supplies I carry off with me. I'll be glad t' sign vouchers so nobody comes up short on my account."

"You're sure about all this?" a man named Glen Adams asked.

"No, sir." Longarm smiled. "But I will be before I go an' arrest anybody." He stood and rubbed his hands together. "Now who's for a drink? I'm buyin'."

Chapter 19

The horses Longarm came up with were of average size and quality. There was a leggy brown that looked pretty decent except for having a narrow chest that suggested it would not have great stamina. He would ride that one himself. The boy was mounted on a short, fat pinto that was a mite on the lazy side but was considered kid proof. It likely wouldn't take a notion to blow up underneath the boy.

The saddles were a pair of castoff cavalry McClellans. Longarm was accustomed to those anyway and made no objection, never mind that they were miserably uncomfortable sons of bitches. Nut-crackers. Ball-busters. Cavalry troopers called them that . . . and a host of less pleasant things as well. But the army saddles were easy on horses, and that was what was needed on long campaigns far from civilization or resupply. There was a very good likelihood that Longarm and Petey Sanderson could expect an extended campaign of their own.

In fact, Longarm hoped they would.

The men who took Mrs. Sanderson and the girl would have to stay clear of towns as long as the women were alive to tell on them. If they were wallowing around in the hog ranches nearby, that would only mean the women were

71

already dead. Longarm was hoping he could find them still living.

Once he had the horses and saddles they could live with, Longarm gathered up some trail supplies and a burro to carry those. He also borrowed a Winchester rifle. The Winchester was chambered in a grizzly-stomping caliber, and a half hour spent out behind the express company barn showed him that it was spot-on accurate.

He thought long and hard about the advisability of putting a gun in the hands of a ten-year-old boy. This ten-year-old had been through plenty in his young life, though, and Longarm needed his help to find and identify both the kidnappers and their victims.

Without Petey to point a finger and say, "Yes, that's them," Longarm would have no chance to figure out who the men were . . . particularly if they'd already killed the two women.

The result of his pondering was that he borrowed a slide-action Colt Lightning in .22 rimfire caliber. The little gun was light and there was no recoil when it fired, no need for a kid to flinch when he shot it. Yet the tiny bullets could do real damage—to game for the pot or to a grownup human being. Longarm figured it would be the perfect weapon for a kid.

The boy's eyes lit up like lanterns when Longarm handed it to him. "Is this mine, sir, for really and true?"

"Whether you keep it or not depends on how you handle it. You said your pa taught you t' shoot, so pay attention to the things he said an' be careful. I bought a good supply o' .22 ammunition an' in the evenings when we make camp, I'll want you to spend some time shooting that gun. You might could need it, an' if you do, I want you to know how to handle it."

"Yes, sir. Thank you, sir."

"I'm gonna put you in charge of the burro, Petey," Longarm said as he loaded the fuzzy-eared little animal. "Lead it behind you, but remember it won't be able to run as fast as the horses, so if we get into a runnin' gunfight or have t' chase their horses, you just let go of the lead rope. The burro will follow along on its own or maybe it won't, but either way I don't want it slowing us down when the time come for us t' run." He jammed a cheroot between his teeth and looked the boy in the eye. "People is more important than things, kid, an' all this burro is carryin' is things. The burro an' everything on it can be replaced. You an' your mama and sister can't. So don't fret yourself overmuch about this animal if he get into a tight spot."

"How will I know when to do what?" the boy asked.

Longarm smiled. "You'll know, son. If we get ourselves in a jam, you will damn sure know it."

"Yes, sir. If you say so."

"Come along now. We need to stop at Mrs. Hayes's house so you can tell her good-bye." The truth was that there was someone in that house he wanted to tell good-bye also, but he did not want to embarrass Jennie Williard by approaching her in public. It was possible folks around here would think the girl was getting uppity and be hard on her because of that. He did, however, hope to find an opportunity to give her a hug and a kiss before they rode out. She was a good girl, and he liked her more than a little.

Longarm looked at their hastily assembled outfit and at the wide-eyed boy who was his partner in their venture. This was not exactly the sort of thing he was used to, but it would just have to do.

"Come along, Petey. A late start is better than none." Longarm took the reins of his brown, and waited for a moment while the boy sorted out his reins and the lead rope to the burro. Then he led the way out to the edge of town to Mrs. Hayes's place.

73

And to sweet Jennie.

It seemed a shame that he couldn't take the time to slip around to her little house and get something more than a chaste hug by way of a good-bye, but duty called. Unfortunately.

Chapter 20

"How do you go about chasing somebody, Longarm?" the boy asked once they were on their way. He was not yet accustomed to riding anyway, and the pinto was fat and wide. What with Petey's short legs and wide seat, he had little grip and bounced like an India rubber ball whenever he got into a trot. Longarm thought he looked funny as hell bouncing along atop the pinto, but of course said nothing about that. And he had to give the boy credit; he never complained about the discomfort.

"You start at the beginning, of course," Longarm said, looking back over his shoulder toward the boy and the stocky pinto, the burro trailing placidly along behind. "We'll go back to your family's wagon. Might be hard on you t' see all that again, but I need t' take a look there. See if I find anything that'll tell me who these men are or where they're going."

He thought it best to not mention that seeing the looted wagon would also allow him to verify that Peter Sanderson was telling the truth and not just spouting a whopper in an attempt to gain sympathy. The boy did not seem the sort to do that. Longarm believed his story about the kidnapping. But a little verification never hurt anybody.

"I'll see what we can learn there, then try t' pick up whatever trail they might've left. It will do a world o' good if they left tracks that I can point to an' know that they belong to the men we want t' trail."

He lit a cheroot, taking the smoke deep and savoring the taste of it. A light breeze whipped the exhaled smoke away. "It's a funny thing about tracking," Longarm said. "Once you get good an' familiar with a particular set o' tracks, you can practically pick them out of a whole herd."

"Are you tracking me now from when I came here?" Petey asked.

"Lord, no. Somebody afoot don't hardly leave any sign, especially somebody small an' light like you are. An' don't let anybody tell you otherwise. There's some as claim to be wizards as trackers. There's even some that really are. But they likely ain't following actual footprints so much as working out how the thing they're tracking thinks, then going that way too."

"What about those men?" Petey asked.

"They shouldn't be so awful hard to track, even out here on the big grass. Horses leave better tracks than men afoot. An' you said your folks had a team of heavy cobs to pull the wagon. Heavy horses leave deep tracks. That should help us get a notion as to which way they went."

They rode in silence for several miles. Then Petey piped up with a question Longarm did not want to answer, even though he'd suspected it would be asked. "If you can't track me from before I came here, how do you know where to go to find our wagon now, Longarm?"

"Guesswork and a lawman's instinct," Longarm said.

It was a bald-faced lie, plain and simple. The truth was that he had been told the general direction. Now he was looking for buzzards.

Petey had said he scraped a little soil over his father's body. That would not have been enough to keep the flies from finding it. Even if there was enough dirt to keep

76

them from reaching the body, they would be swarming over it. And wherever the flies congregate, the buzzards soon follow.

Buzzards overhead should pinpoint the spot for Longarm. They would be visible from miles away.

That would lead him to the wagon. His problem then would be to keep Petey from coming close and seeing what was left of his pa. Because while the flies might not be able to penetrate a covering of soil, the buzzards, coyotes, and foxes damn sure could. By now there was not likely to be a whole hell of a lot left of John Sanderson, and what there was would not be pretty to look at. For certain sure Longarm did not want the boy to see his father's body that way.

Late that afternoon it was time for him to come up with another lie. A flight of buzzards drifting gracefully in the air led him across the rolling grass to a forlorn abandoned wagon sitting in the bottom of a shallow swale.

"That's it," Petey said, a hint of excitement in his voice. And a hint of sadness too. "That's my papa's outfit."

Before they came too close, Longarm turned away.

"Where are we going? I thought you said—"

"We're gonna set up our camp over here. I don't want us an' our horses trampling over any sign that's been left down there. So what I figure t' do is, the two of us will make camp. Then while you tend to the horses an' finish laying our blankets out, I'm gonna walk over to the wagon an' see what I can find in the way of helpful sign."

"Can't I come too?"

"No. Flat-out no. You don't know about tracking an' you're apt t' mess up something without even knowing you're doin' it. I know you wouldn't do anything deliberate, but you could do something by accident, something that would help me if only I could've seen it. Best that we don't take that chance, boy."

"I'd be real careful."

"No," Longarm said, his voice sharp.

77

"Are you just trying to keep me from seeing what's there? Because I already seen it, you know. I'm the one that buried my pap. I already seen him dead."

"Yes, you have," Longarm agreed. But you haven't seen his body the way it is now after the scavengers have worked it over, he could have added. "I told you what the reason is. So unless you figure you know more about this tracking business than I do, you'd best do what you're told and stay clear."

The boy looked resigned but not defiant. He dropped his chin and looked like he might want to pout a little, but he kept his mouth shut, and once Longarm decided on a likely spot for them to bed down for the night, Petey pitched in and did his share of the camp chores and then some.

"Did you help your pa on the way out here?"

"Yes, sir. I made the fire and fed the horses and like. Papa took care of brushing them and checking their feet 'cause I wasn't big enough for those things. Wasn't tall enough to curry their backs nor strong enough to hold their hoofs up while I picked rocks out of their feet. But I could do most everything else that needed done. I helped out. We all did."

"Then you can do those things for our camps too," Longarm said.

"Do you think it will take long for us to catch them?"

"They've been gone from here a good many days already, but since they have your womenfolk with them, they may well've decided to settle in one spot for a spell. You and me will just have t' do our best, Petey, an' figure this hunt will take however long it takes. That's about all we can do."

"And after we catch them?"

"I'll arrest them. Take them in for trial. Likely they'll hang, although if they get a good lawyer, they might get off with prison terms instead."

"If they get hanged, can I watch?"

"Would you want to?"

"Yes, sir, I would. They're mean and they're awful and they shot my pa and I hate them. I hope they hang until their guts fall out. I hope they hang and I see it when they do."

"Then I'll try an' arrange it that you can watch, Petey." He blew out a puff of smoke, then shrugged. "If they hang."

"Promise?"

Longarm nodded. "It's a promise."

"Thank you, sir."

"Go ahead an' finish up with the chores here, son. I'm gonna walk across the hill to where that wagon is. We'll have something to eat when I get back."

"Yes, sir. I'll have everything ready."

Longarm took a look around and saw nothing alarming, nothing that would jeopardize the boy's safety—a boy, he reminded himself, who had buried his father and walked alone in search of the killers with nothing but a pocketknife and a lot of determination—then set off toward the wagon on the other side of the hill.

Chapter 21

Longarm was glad the boy would never have to see what the birds and the small creatures had done to his father's body. John Sanderson was barely recognizable as having been a human thing, never mind what he'd looked like. There just wasn't much left of him. What there was, Longarm left alone, making no attempt to bury the remains again.

Instead, he lit a cheroot and very slowly, very carefully walked around and around the Sanderson wagon in ever-decreasing circles, coming closer and closer to the wagon itself and examining every footprint or hoofprint he could find in the process.

Most of the tracks close to the wagon were overlapping, one on top of another, having been made by eight different people, all of them moving around within a fairly small space close to the wagon. That jumble of scrapes and indentations told him little.

Out a little distance away from the wagon was another matter entirely. There he was able to find three well-defined hoofprints made by light horses and one good print by a large hoof. That would have been one of the Sanderson animals from their team. Four complete prints undisturbed by having been walked over was more than he hoped for. Those four he would recognize if he saw them again, he thought. Hoped.

When he was satisfied with that, he went back to the wagon and closely examined the ring of stones where some member of the family, likely Petey, had built a fire that last night his family was together.

At least one person who had been there chewed cheap tobacco. At least one smoked cheap rum crooks. Longarm reminded himself to ask Petey if his father had been fond of either of those.

The light was already fading from the western sky by the time Longarm got inside the wagon itself. Just as Petey said, the rig had been ransacked. The floorboards had been torn up, suggesting that if Sanderson kept any cash hidden, it had been found by the kidnappers before they were done with their devilment. That was something else Longarm wanted to ask Petey about.

He was able to get a good idea about the sizes of the two Sanderson women by the clothing that was left behind. He also took what clothing of Petey's he could find, wadding the garments into a ball and tying them with some twine so he could carry them easily.

Nothing of any real value had been left behind other than the wagon itself, and the kidnappers probably reasoned—correctly—that a wagon is a helluva lot easier to track than a horse. Harder to maneuver too. A horse can usually find a way down into a gully and back out on the other side, while a wagon might well be stopped cold and have to go miles out of the way to get across.

Once he had learned all he was going to, he went to the back end of the rig and put a shoulder to the tailgate. He began to push.

Getting the damned thing to begin rolling was the hard part. Once it started moving, it was fairly easy to keep it going.

He pushed it about a dozen feet until it stood beside John Sanderson's desecrated body. Then he went forward to the side, bent his knees, took a good hold on the underside of the wagon body, and began to lift.

It took some doing, but Longarm was able to topple the wagon onto its side. It went over with a loud clatter. After that, it seemed no effort at all was required to push it the rest of the way over so that it rested upside down on top of Sanderson's grave.

Puffing more than a little from exertion, Longarm sat for a moment on the underside of the overturned outfit. He finished his cheroot and ground the butt underfoot, then took out a match.

When Longarm walked back to his and Petey's camp, he left the wagon blazing as a funeral pyre over Sanderson's grave. The burned-out hulk of the wagon and the ash that was left behind should act as a deterrent and keep most of the scavengers away. Young Petey need never know.

He reminded himself to ask the boy what those horses looked like. And there was something else he intended to . . . oh, yes. The tobacco. He needed to know if John Sanderson used tobacco and if so in what form.

Those were little enough things, Longarm knew, but it is the little details that add up to a whole.

The night air was becoming chilly. Longarm lengthened his stride.

Chapter 22

"We're getting closer," Longarm commented. He was squatting on his heels beside the cold remains of a fire.

"How's come you would say that? We've only come ten or twelve miles," Petey said.

Longarm picked up a stick and used the tip of it to stir through the fire pit. "Look how much ash there is. An' these bones. Antelope maybe. Point is, they was here three or four days before they decided t' move on. Maybe a mite longer."

"You can tell all that?"

He nodded. "Pay attention to the world that's around you, boy. Think about what you see. Take this here, for instance." He prodded some scorched and fire-blackened bones with the stick. "Ribs. What does that tell you, Petey?"

The kid shrugged. "I dunno. That they liked to eat ribs?"

Longarm ruffled the boy's hair. "Everybody likes ribs. No, what I'm getting at is that men who are intent on moving don't take the time to separate out the ribs and pull them apart like this. Men in a hurry don't really butcher their kill. They cut off chunks of meat, roast it, an' move along. These ol' boys took the time to roast these racks o' ribs using those rocks right there. You see the grease there? An' there? That was laid down over several days. Or anyway several times cooking meat, an' I can't see six people eating so much that they'd cook all that for one meal."

"You can tell all that?"

Longarm nodded. "If you pay attention, you can."

"Are we going to stop here too?"

Longarm looked toward the west where the sun would soon disappear. And where the kidnappers already had vanished. "I reckon it's late enough that we can go ahead an' make camp."

"Can I practice with my rifle, sir?"

"Better than that, you can walk out on that hill there an' bring us back some meat for the pot tonight. I seen some prairie chickens fluttering about. Whyn't you go shoot us a couple of them. They'd taste good for a change."

"What about? . . ."

"I'll take care o' the fire. You go fetch our dinner."

"Yes, *sir*." The boy grabbed his .22 out of the saddle boot he had fashioned from some scraps of canvas. He checked the loads in the little rifle the way Longarm had shown him, then trotted happily off in the direction Longarm indicated.

When Petey was well out into the grass, Longarm again hunkered down beside the fire and poked into the charred bits. He found the one he wanted, the one he had spotted earlier, and picked it up.

It was—or had been—cloth. With a ruffle at one edge. Woman stuff obviously. And there was blood on it.

"Not much for travelin' long distances, are they," Longarm remarked when they reached another campsite that pretty surely was left by the kidnappers. It was only twenty-odd miles from the last one. With no wagon to slow them down, they should have been covering thirty miles or so each day. Forty if they wanted to push hard. More if they cared nothing about their horses. The army consistently traveled forty miles a day, and that was with no spare horses to change onto.

86

"Can you figure out why they'd choose t' stop here?" Longarm asked.

The kid climbed down off his pinto and peered carefully into the fire pit. After several minutes he shook his head. "No, sir, I can't."

Longarm pointed to the north. "Look over there. See that smoke? There's a small town or a helluva big ranch over there. Likely they wanted t' do some trading at a store. Buy some liquor, I'd guess. Why do I say that? Because o' that broken whiskey bottle over there." He pointed again at some shards of glass. "Likely they ran out of whiskey. Now they'd want an opportunity to buy some." He took out a cheroot, lit it, and shook the match out before he continued.

"They couldn't just ride in an' be seen holding two women captive. Your mama and Betty would holler for help if there was decent folk around. So the men had t' hold the women out here while some split off to ride over the ridge there an' do their trading. What else can you make out from this fire?"

The boy looked at the cold ashes for quite a while, then said, "They only stayed here one night before they moved on."

"Why d'you think that?"

"Because there isn't much ash and there's no bones left in this fire like there was back at the other place."

"Good. You're paying attention. I like that."

The boy beamed at Longarm's praise.

"Now you and me," Longarm said, "are gonna ride over there an' see what we can learn from whoever is where that smoke is rising. Those kidnappers had t' mostly stay outa sight because of your mama and your sister, but we ain't restricted like that, and we ain't gonna have to cook for ourselves tonight. Come along now. Let's see what we can find."

"Yes, sir." Petey pulled the burro's head up and bumped the pinto with his heels.

Chapter 23

"Those are Pa's horses. Those four standing back there." The animals were as Petey had described days ago. Longarm was not surprised. "Let's get them back, kid."

"If you say so."

"You got little enough in this world, boy, and those horses are worth something. Come along now."

They found the proprietor of the feed supply outfit that owned the horses now. Or thought he did.

"My name is Caldwell. What can I do for you?" Longarm introduced himself and explained something of the situation. "Sorry," Caldwell said. "I understand what you're telling me, mister, but I bought those horses fair and square. They're mine now." He shrugged. "I'm afraid it's just the boy's tough luck."

Caldwell was a big man. He stood there like a small mountain, his expression set and unyielding. He hooked his thumbs into the shoulder straps of his overalls and rocked slightly on the balls of his feet. The man was a brawler, Longarm suspected, and not in any mood for charity toward a family he did not know. "I'll tell you all I can . . . what little there is of it . . . about the men I bought those animals off of, but I bought 'em fair. Paid top dollar for them too."

Longarm smiled. "For your sake, mister, I hope you're stretching the truth about that. I hope you didn't pay much for them because you won't be getting any of it back."

"Hey now, I should be entitled to a fair return on my investment."

"Mr. Caldwell, you bought stolen property. I could run you in as an accessory to robbery an' to murder too. Instead, I'm gonna assume you didn't know the truth an' let you off. But the horses belong to the boy."

Petey tugged at Longarm's sleeve, but the tall lawman ignored him for the moment. He was fairly sure the boy would just try to avoid a confrontation by giving up his claim on the horses.

"I say they already belong to me."

"An' I say I have the authority t' put you behind bars while a judge works out all those little details." That was stretching the truth until it screamed, but Longarm had a point and damn sure intended to make it. "What I can do," he went on, "is to give you a voucher for keeping the animals. Fifteen cents per head per day. I can do that because they're material evidence in a capital crime."

"Fifteen cents my ass!" Caldwell protested. "I charge fifty cents to board a horse. More for heavy sons of bitches like those."

"The government pays fifteen cents. I'll make sure you get what you're entitled to out of it. I want you t' keep them till the boy and his mama come back to claim them. An' I want them t' be sound the next time I see them. Do I see a single rib showing on any one of them, friend, I personally will whip your ass until you holler uncle."

"You aren't man enough to do that."

Longarm grinned. "I'm kinda busy now, but I'd be willin' to, as they say, engage in a sporting pursuit with you when I get back here."

"I got fifty pounds on you, mister."

"An' I got a whole lot o' meanness on you."

90

"By God, maybe you have at that."

"Trust me. I do. So take good care o' the boy's horses for him while he's gone. The United States government will pay you for it. Now let's set down an' you can tell me everything you know about the men we're trailin'. What are their names, fer instance. Did they say where they're bound? How far ahead of us would you say they'll be now? I want t' know everything you can think of, starting with how many showed up here the day you thought you bought those horses."

To the boy he said, "If you like, Petey, I can give you some money so you can go over to the mercantile an' buy yourself something."

"No, sir. I want to hear this too."

"All right, son. I reckon you're entitled to that much. We talk with this gentleman here an' then go get us a good dinner for a change."

Chapter 24

Longarm and Petey bought supplies, had dinner, had a shoe reset on Petey's pinto, and slept that night in real beds in a clean and pleasant boardinghouse. By the time they were done, Longarm had had a chance to speak with at least half the merchants in the community to gain their impressions of the three men who had showed up one day to sell those wagon horses.

"I'm worried," the boy said as they rode out after an early breakfast the next morning.

"'Bout what, kid?"

"My mama. My crazy old sister. Those men . . . the man at the store back there said they bought shotgun shells. I heard him say that. Do you think they're planning to kill my mama and my sister?"

Longarm rode in silence for a considerable time before he answered. At length, he responded, "I expect they probably would kill them eventually, Petey. What you and me got to hope for is that those evil men are still enjoying having the women for . . . for slaves."

"But *why*?"

"Why what?"

"Why would they want them for slaves? Couldn't they cook for themselves and clean up?"

"Sure, but some fellas . . . it makes them feel good to have something or somebody that they can lord it over. That's the sort of man would kick a stray dog for no reason. Or would want a slave to order around an' punish if something wasn't done to his satisfaction." That was not exactly a complete answer, but Longarm did not think it should be up to him to educate young Peter Sanderson about sex.

A little while later, Petey observed, "We aren't following their tracks."

"No, we ain't," Longarm agreed. "We'll keep going west 'cause that's the direction Chuck and Barney"—names they had heard attributed to the men in town—"an' the other two are headed. You might notice that we're kinda bending a little south of west. That's because I figure eventually we should cut their trail. Assumin' they stay to the same general course as before. If they didn't, then we'll just curl all the way back. But sooner or later we'll see their tracks again. I'll keep after them till we do."

"I thought a tracker followed the footprints of whoever he was tracking."

"This is quicker," Longarm said.

"Is there *any*thing you can't do, Mr. Marshal?"

Longarm smiled. "Damn right. You wouldn't want t' eat an apple pie I baked. Nor wear a shirt I sewed."

After a bit, Petey said, "My mama bakes an awful fine pie. Why, her rhubarb pie is the best there ever was." He straightened up tall in his saddle and smiled. "I remember . . ." Then his expression crumbled and he looked like he was on the verge of tears as he remembered his mother and the home they had left to chase the dream of rich, free farmland in the West, the home where once she had baked rhubarb pie for her son Petey.

Petey ran his fingers lightly over the butt of the little .22 rifle.

Thinking about getting those four murderers in the sights of that rifle, Longarm figured.

That evening, as they settled down beside their campfire with canned beans and some fresh pork they bought in that last town, Longarm said, "Why don't you break out another box of cartridges for your rifle, kid. Walk over there far enough you won't spook the horses an' have a little target practice."

"Yes, *sir!*" The boy jumped to his feet and dug into the pack where his ammunition was kept. Target practice was something he was always eager to do. Unlike certain camp chores.

"Don't shoot the whole box, Petey. Remember t' keep a full magazine in the rifle. Just in case."

"Yes, sir." The boy was grinning when he scampered to do what Longarm told him to.

Typical kid, Longarm figured.

Longarm just hoped the boy wasn't completely an orphan now because he was right about one thing. The mother was older and undoubtedly less attractive than the sister. And Betty was quite capable of handling the minor camp chores without her mother's help. If the woman pissed those four off, they would very likely kill her on the spot. Maybe already had.

Bastards! he thought, his expression in that moment turning hard as chiseled granite. It would not have been healthy for any adult human person to cross him at a time like that.

Chapter 25

Longarm had calmed down come daybreak and a cold meal taken in the saddle. It helped his disposition considerably when a good hour short of mid-morning they cut the hoofprints they were looking for.

After stopping to examine the trail, Longarm grunted and said, "This is them. Looks like they picked up a pack mule in town. Maybe some spare horses too as there seems t' be enough tracks to account for the four men plus your ma an' sister and one left over. That's why I figure they're pulling a packhorse just like we have your burro."

"Can you tell how far ahead they are?"

"A day, day an' a half maybe," Longarm said.

"We're gaining on them."

"Ayuh. We'll catch up to them, boy. Make no mistake about it. We damn sure *will* catch up to them."

About an hour later, still following in the tracks of the kidnappers, Longarm pointed to some dust rising to the south of their westward-trending path.

"Is that them?" Petey asked, rising in his stirrups and reaching for the .22 rifle that dangled from his saddle.

"Calm down, boy. Ain't no way that could be them. It's way too soon. From the wrong direction too. But it could

97

be that they've seen those men an' your women. We'll ask them."

Fifteen minutes later, the dust revealed itself to be coming not from a group of riders, but from the wheels of a pair of heavy freight wagons. Their course was northerly while Longarm and the boy were riding west. If both continued without change, Longarm and Petey would cross well ahead of the slower wagons. Instead, Longarm reined south away from the tracks left by the kidnappers.

"Let's talk to them, Petey. It ain't likely they've seen our crowd but it can't hurt to ask." He grinned. "Besides, it's nigh onto dinnertime and their cook is sure as hell bound t' be better than ours." He put his brown into a lope.

Petey laughed and gigged his pinto to keep up with Longarm.

They were within a couple hundred yards of the wagons when the first white puffball showed beside the driving box on the second wagon. The dull boom of the gunshot was not heard until several seconds later. Longarm never did hear where the bullet went.

"Is that? . . ."

"Yes, it is," Longarm said. "Rein away. Quick."

He needn't have worried. Petey had already turned the pinto north, away from the wagons.

"Not that way," Longarm said. "We'll go around to the south of them."

"Wouldn't it be quicker to stay . . ." But by then Longarm had already spurred the brown south. Petey yanked the pinto around and followed.

A rifle in the lead wagon boomed, and this time the sizzle of the passing slug was close enough to hear. The boy ducked, even though by then the bullet was well past.

Longarm slowed his horse and motioned Petey up beside him. "No, boy. Over here on this side. Get me between you an' them wagons. I don't reckon they're actual trying to shoot us, just t' keep us away, but it never hurts t' be safe."

"It sh-sh-sure sounds to me like they're trying to hit us," Petey stammered.

Another shot rang out, from the second wagon again, and this time the strike of the bullet was close enough to kick dirt onto the legs of the burro. The little animal spooked, and for a moment Longarm thought it would pull Petey and the pinto down.

"Dammit!" he barked.

The rifle in the lead wagon fired again as well, the slug passing just above Longarm's head.

"Run 'em, Petey."

Longarm held back, wanting to match his pace to that of the pinto so he could shield the boy. After a moment, the two of them managed to synchronize the speeds of their mounts, and Longarm led the way around to the south of the moving wagons.

When they were immediately behind the wagons, Longarm pulled the brown to a halt. Petey ran on a few seconds until he realized Longarm was no longer beside him. Then he stopped and came back.

"What're you doing?"

"There's bound t' be a reason why them fellas started shooting like they done. I figure t' find out what it is." He smiled. "Besides, kid, it's illegal t' shoot at a federal officer. Don't you know that? I'm perfectly within my rights t' investigate those ol' boys an' to arrest their asses if I don't like what they have to say."

"How are you going to do that, sir?"

Longarm's smile turned into a wide grin. "Why, Peter, I'm gonna deputize you and you are gonna help me."

"Yes, *sir*!" The boy again reached for the butt of his .22.

Chapter 26

"What I want you t' do, Petey, is t' put the spurs to that lit-tle pinto an' run out wide. Wide now, mind you. I don't want you in close enough so that they can see you're a boy. I want them worryin' about what it is you're up to out there." Longarm grinned. "An' what that will be is a decoy. I hope you don't mind me using you for bait, but you're what I got. Okay?"

"Yes, sir. Are you serious about making me your deputy?"

"Yes, I am." That was a little detail he would certainly have omitted, it having no legal effect whatsoever, but ob-viously it was important to the boy. "Raise your right hand and repeat after me."

Longarm gave the kid a perfectly normal swearing in— Peter was, what, ten years old—then sent him off at full speed, the little burro scampering along behind for all he was worth.

He gave Petey time to make a rough quarter circle out to where the men on the wagons should be worrying about him getting ahead. Then Longarm threw the steel to the brown and put it into a dead run for the ass end of the trail-ing wagon. He held the Winchester he had borrowed from

Jason Bradley back when they started on this odyssey to find and rescue Petey's family. If the men on the wagons saw him back there, they should see the Winchester too. Might make them think a little before they did any indiscriminate shooting at strangers.

A puff of white smoke appeared from within the covered body of the trail wagon and a slug whined nearby, then another.

The brown shied. Longarm yanked its head back around and spurred it again.

He was within twenty yards or less from the tailgate of the wagon when another shot struck the brown square on the forehead and it went crashing down, dead before it hit the ground. Longarm rolled free, the Winchester still in his hand.

He rolled back again, lying prone behind the dead horse with his rifle barrel propped on its flank. He fired, levered the rifle, and fired again, aiming not into the back of the wagon but underneath it. At the front of the rig a horse screamed and went down with a shattered ankle. Longarm took careful aim and put the horse out of its misery.

He crawled out to the side to get an unobstructed view and quickly fired again, dropping one horse in the traces of the lead wagon. He rolled back into the protection of the dead brown's body.

"You sonuvabitch," a voice complained from inside one of the wagons.

"I'm not the one as started shooting, mister," Longarm said, raising his voice but not his head. "Now we both know you ain't going anywhere until you get down an' spend some time cutting those downed horses outa the harness, an' when you do that I got you dead in my sights. Reckon you can surrender now or I can kill you later. You decide."

"You don't have to sound so pleased about it."

"I'll try an' sound sad if it'll make you feel any better," Longarm shouted back.

"All right, dammit. We give up."

"Fine. Leave your guns where they are. Get down an' stand over there ten yards or thereabouts west o' your rigs. Do it *now*!"

"You don't hafta get huffy 'bout it."

"Mister, I got some ants crawling on my shirt tryin' to find a way in. That means I ain't gonna be willing to lay here very much longer. An' if I have to come up there after you, you ain't gonna like the result. I'm guessing that a man can't see much daylight from inside a pine box that's six feet underground."

"All right, all right, we're coming."

Two men showed themselves. They climbed down onto the bare grass and, unarmed, walked out to the side where they stood waiting for Longarm to collect them.

When Longarm walked forward to take the men into custody, he saw the boy with his pinto and the burro on station to the front of the wagons. Longarm had not given the kid instructions beyond acting as a distraction. Instead, he and his little .22 were in position to block the wagons had they tried to make their escape in that direction.

Damned spunky kid, Longarm thought.

Chapter 27

"Aw, shit," the nearer of the men grumbled when he saw Longarm's badge.

"Your tough luck," Longarm responded cheerfully. "Keep your eye on 'em, Deputy," he said to Petey, who had brought the pinto and the burro up, And the .22 rifle.

Longarm walked over to the wagons, and quickly saw why the men had not wanted to be stopped. Especially by an officer of the law. He lit a cheroot and walked back to the dejected pair, who were sitting cross-legged on the ground.

"Headed for one of the Indian reservations, was you?" he asked, his voice pleasant enough.

"No sirree bob. That would be illegal," one of the prisoners answered.

To Petey, Longarm explained. "Those wagons is filled with casks of alcohol, son. They can cut it with creek water an' add some crap for coloring an' a little flavor. Next thing you know they've got three, four times as much volume and call it whiskey. That much whiskey would bring a helluva price on one o' the reservations up Dakota way." He turned his attention back to his prisoners. "An' that is exactly the direction these old boys was headed when they started shooting at a deputy United States marshal." Longarm walked closer to the men and bent down so that he was staring hard into their faces. "Ain't that so, boys."

"We wasn't doing nothing."

"You damn sure shot at me. That right there is a federal offense."

"Look, can't we make this thing go away? All part as friends, huh? It'd be worth, say, fifty dollars. Cash money."

"You killed my horse," Longarm said.

"All right, make it a hundred dollars. There's a town right over yonder. Macklin. It's only about five miles across those hills. You can buy you a decent horse over there for twenty dollars or so an' have some left over to party with. Or whatever."

"Two hundred," the other man quickly said. It earned him a dirty look from his partner, who obviously was trying to hold their costs down.

"Shit, George, the last fella got two hundred."

George rolled his eyes. "Shut the fuck up, Larry. Jesus Christ!"

Longarm chuckled. "You're offering me two hundred, Larry? To pretend none o' this ever happened?"

"I never said that, did I?" the scruffy fellow named Larry countered.

"Actually, I believe you did," Longarm said. "Pretty much." He pursed his lips and spat. Then he grinned. "That means I get t' charge you with attempted bribery. You heard them didn't you, Deputy?"

"Yes, sir, I surely did."

"Keep in mind what you heard, son. Could be you'll have to testify to it in a court o' law."

Longarm motioned with the barrel of his Winchester. "Get up, you two. You got some work t' do. First thing, I want you t' fetch my gear off'n that dead horse back there. Then you'll need t' cut those dead horses outa harness an' get your rigs ready to roll again. We're all of us going over to this Macklin place so's I can turn you in for prosecution an' get on about our business. Which you bastards done interrupted."

Chapter 28

Macklin wasn't much, but it was bigger than the last town they had seen, and it had both a jail and a telegraph. Longarm stopped their odd train — he had chained the two wagons together and put all six remaining draft horses into one hitch—on the street in front of the jail. He climbed down from the driving box.

The two prisoners were handcuffed and sitting on whiskey kegs in the back of the first wagon.

"Turn around an' set facing backward on the seat, Petey."

The kid did what he was told without questioning why he should.

"I want you t' keep an eye on these buzzards. If either of them moves or tries to get away . . . shoot the son of a bitch."

"Are you serious, sir?"

"Dead serious." He peered inside the wagon and said, "Did you boys hear that? You move and the kid here will fill your backsides with lead."

"We ain't going anywhere."

"Damn right you ain't."

Longarm stepped inside the town marshal's office. There

were two men there, seated on opposite sides of a battered desk. A checkerboard lay between them.

"Is one o' you gents the marshal here?"

"That'd be me," a lean man with a mustache almost as splendid as Longarm's said. He stood. "Tom Carter's my name. This here is my deputy, Joseph Morton. How can we help you?"

Longarm introduced himself and said, "I got a couple prisoners out here that you could take off my hands. I'm on the trail of a gang o' kidnappers an' got no time to fuck around with a pair of whiskey peddlers. I'd consider it a favor was you t' take them off my hands an' deliver them down to Denver for me. Naturally, the fed'ral gov'ment will pay for their upkeep and transport."

Carter looked at his deputy and said, "There you go, Joey. Escorting prisoners will get you some mileage pay along with your salary."

"How much extra, Tom?"

"However much I say." The town marshal turned his attention back to Longarm. "There. That's taken care of. Is there anything else you need?"

"Matter o' fact there is. I got a couple confiscated wagons out here loaded with alcohol not yet made up into whiskey. Those need t' be sold an' the proceeds turned over to the federal gov'ment. I'd like you t' handle that too. For a reasonable fee, o' course."

"I can do that, sure."

"Last thing, I'll need to get an advance on the proceeds from that sale. I got t' buy a horse to replace one the whiskey peddlers shot out from under me."

"Mixed it up with them, did you?" Carter asked.

"Some. But we worked it out."

"I'm surprised you brought them in still breathing. There's a lot of officers would've cut them down and been done with it."

"Maybe, but I ain't one o' those."

Carter stood. He said, "Joey, let's go help the marshal get himself in order here. Lead the way, Long. We're right behind you."

Petey looked disappointed that he'd had no chance to shoot anyone, but he turned his charges over to Deputy Morton when Longarm gave him the word. Morton took them inside the jail while Carter led the wagons to a livery on the edge of town.

"The marshal here needs a horse," he told the hostler who was there forking fresh hay into stalls that already had been cleaned. "What is available?"

The man nodded toward one of the stalls. "You can have him. He's all I got that I'd be willing to sell."

"Remember what you and Chuckie were doing out by the creek last month?"

"Yes, sir."

Carter turned to Longarm and said, "You can take any animal in the place." He looked back at the hostler and repeated, "Any of them that you see. Any."

Later, after Longarm had chosen a handsome bay and led it outside, Petey asked, "What do you think that man was caught doing to make him back down like that?"

Longarm grinned. "I dunno, son, but he *sure* don't want it spoken around."

He fetched his saddle and bridle out of the trailing wagon and fussed over them until he was satisfied they fit the bay properly, then said, "We need to get us a meal that we ain't cooked ourselves. Then I want to send a wire to my boss down in Denver. Tell him what we're up to and where."

Over a plate of eggs and pan-fried steak, the boy asked, "Sir, do you really think my mother is still alive?"

Longarm grunted. "I got no way to know for sure, Petey, but you an' me are gonna keep right on *believing* that she is. Her and Betty too. An' we're gonna keep right after them in

111

the belief that they're alive and that us two will catch up with them."

"Can I shoot those men when we catch them?" the kid asked.

"Only if you got to, son. Only if you got to."

Chapter 29

As they prepared to bed down in Macklin's only hotel, the boy pulled his trousers off, then stood in the middle of the small room with them trailing from his left hand.

"Something wrong, Petey?" Longarm asked.

"Yes, sir. But I don't know if it's anything I should bother you with."

Longarm shrugged. "Tell me. If nothing else that'll get it off your chest, and if it's nothing to worry about, then I won't be bothered an' neither will you."

"Well, sir, you know how nobody pays attention to a kid."

"True enough," Longarm admitted.

"And this afternoon. When you was talking with Marshal Carter, those two men looked all worried and repen . . . uh . . ."

"Repentant?"

"Yes, sir. That's the word. They looked real repentant when you and Marshal Carter was talking at them. But when you looked away, they was winking at Deputy Morton and making silly faces. Then when they thought you might see, they got looks like they was pledging they'd straighten out and be good."

"You saw them do that?"

"Yes, sir. A couple times. Did I do the right thing to tell you that?"

"You sure did, Petey. You damn sure did." Longarm reversed the process of undressing, leaning down and pulling his boots back on.

"You want me to get dressed, sir?"

"No. I want you to shuck your clothes and crawl into those blankets. I'm not all that sleepy, so I think I'm gonna go find a drink and a poker game to relax me while I think about what you told me here." Longarm tousled the boy's hair. "Go ahead an' go to sleep. I won't be gone long."

"Yes, sir, if you say so. Sir?"

"Um-hmm?"

"If you're going to play some cards, why is it that you're taking your rifle along?"

"Habit," Longarm told him. "Does it bother you?"

"No, sir. Would it be all right if I sleep with my rifle?"

"Do that, Petey. It'll be perfectly all right with me." He smiled. "Just don't wake up an' shoot me when I come in here in the middle o' the night, all right?"

"I won't, sir. I promise."

"Good enough." Longarm waited until the boy was in bed, then pulled his blanket up under the kid's chin and tucked him in. He got a sleepy smile in return. "G'night, Petey."

"Good night, sir."

Longarm let himself out of the room and walked downstairs to the lobby and on out into the crisp night air. Instead of turning left toward the one good saloon he knew of in town, he turned right, toward the livery. The walk was not far.

When he got there, he saw that lanterns shined bright in the back of the livery barn and there was a bustle of activity despite the hour. Longarm skirted around the side of the barn and stopped in the shadows to observe for a moment.

114

His two prisoners along with Deputy Morton were busily building a hitch in front of the whiskey wagons. The wagons were still chained together the way Longarm had brought them in, one being pulled by the horses while the other was chained behind like a trailer.

He noticed too that the "prisoners" had their revolvers back on their hips.

"It takes you way the hell outa your way, boys," the deputy was telling them, "but if you go all the way over to the Deadwood stage road, you can turn north there and no tracker on the face of this here earth could sort your prints out from all the other traffic on that road."

"That takes too long," the rumpled fellow named George said.

"Not as long as a stretch in the pen," Morton countered. "Now hurry along, will you? I want to be gone from here come daybreak. That son of a bitch Long might not be much for laying in bed once the sun comes up."

"So right you are, boys," Longarm muttered under his breath.

Morton was standing in the driving box trying to straighten out the lines while the other two coaxed the big horses to back up toward the tongue and the traces. The harness was in place and they almost had the whiskey ready to roll.

Longarm stayed where he was, silently watching, while they finished their work. Then George nodded to his partner, Larry, and Larry climbed into the second wagon. Longarm could not see what he did in there, but it took him little time to find the handful of coins he came out with moments later. Larry slowly and carefully counted the coins into Joe Morton's open hand.

Longarm was not close enough to see the coins, but if they were twenty-dollar gold pieces, as seemed likely, then Deputy Morton was receiving the two hundred dollars that had been offered to Longarm.

Whatever the amount, both parties seemed satisfied when they were done.

"I'll ride a ways alongside of you," Morton said, "in case there's anybody sees us. Then you can turn north or go wherever the hell you like. Me, I'm gonna take a little vacation. Go get me some pussy other than my old lady." He laughed.

Longarm suspected the gentleman would not be laughing quite so hard in just a little while.

Chapter 30

The men extinguished the lanterns that had illuminated their work. Shortly afterward, there was the creaking of leather and the jangle of chains. Wheels turned, and the little cavalcade rolled out of town at a swift walk.

Longarm slipped inside the barn and saddled the bay horse. He mounted . . . and damned near came off again. The bay apparently liked to buck a little when first saddled.

Longarm rode him down, then turned the horse's head in the direction the whiskey wagons had gone. He put the bay into an easy lope, and caught up with the wagons in twenty minutes or so. Joseph Morton was still with them.

The night was clear and a pale moon was rising. Out away from town, there was enough visibility to show form if not color.

Morton was riding alongside the wagons. Longarm rode up on the opposite side.

"Evenin', boys. Nice night t' travel, eh?"

"What?"

Longarm thought Larry was going to jump clean out of his britches. Obviously, he hadn't known they were not alone on the road.

"Is that you, Long?"

"It's me, Joe."

"Nice of you to give me a hand with these here prisoners, Long. Thanks. I'm just, uh, taking them down to Cheyenne like the marshal said."

"Always glad t' help a fellow lawman, Joe. But I do have a question for you. How's come George an' Larry here have their sidearms back?"

They all must have known that the game was up, but George was the only one who acted on it. He grabbed for his revolver and swung around toward Longarm.

It was a mistake.

Longarm's hand flashed, and his Colt roared, lighting the scene for one brief instant, the flash of burning gunpowder hanging in the air long enough to illuminate George with a wet, pulsing hole in the side of his head and a spray of dark blood visible on the other side.

Larry screamed and dropped onto the floor of the driving box, covering his head with both arms and whimpering like a kicked pup.

Joe Morton made no immediate attempt to draw his own revolver. His first thought was for escape. He reined his horse away and spurred it down the road, back in the direction of Macklin, where he would know places and people where he could hide.

The wagons with George's body and the cowering Larry likely would not be going far, Longarm figured. But he did not want that bent-shield asshole Morton to escape charges of interfering with a federal prisoner. That should earn him a couple years of breaking rocks, and Longarm intended for the man to get what he earned.

Lawmen on the take always pissed Longarm off more than nearly any other crime; it was something that reflected on every man who carried a badge.

Longarm threw the steel to the bay and braced himself for another round of bucking, but the horse only pinned its ears back and set off after the fleeing Morton.

Apparently the bay had the idea that they were in a race with that other horse. And the bay intended to win. All Longarm had to do was bend down to the bay's neck and let it run. The horse could see far better in the dim light than any human could, so Longarm gave it its head and trusted it to know what was needed.

The bay horse proved to be as swift as it was handsome, catching up with Joe Morton's ewe-necked sorrel within a minute or so.

"Give it up, Morton," Longarm called as he closed in on the galloping sorrel.

"Fuck you, Long. I ain't going into no cell. I put too many into cells my own self to ever want that."

"Then you shouldn't of taken a bribe, you ratfucker."

"I won't let you take me, Long."

"You got no choice." By then Longarm was riding practically at Morton's hip. "You'll go in alive or dead, Morton, but you will by God go in."

"Then it's gotta be dead." Joe Morton drew his pistol.

Longarm's bullet knocked the man out of his saddle. He hit the ground hard, his sorrel racing on without him. He bounced once and rolled onto his back, as lifeless as a rag doll. Longarm reined the bay to a reluctant halt—the horse wanted to keep on after the sorrel—and rode back to Morton's body.

"Wrong choice, old son," Longarm said to the empty husk that had been a man. He dismounted, careful to keep his Colt in hand and an eye on Morton in case the man was playing possum. Not that he believed that, but then he had not stayed on the sunny side of the sod this long by being stupid.

He knelt beside Morton long enough to check the deputy for a pulse. He did not find one.

"Idiot sonuvabitch," he mumbled as he mounted the bay again. He made no attempt to take care of the body. There was no point. He could collect it when he brought Larry and the whiskey wagons back.

He surely did wish, though, that he'd had a chance to talk with Morton. Longarm could not be sure now that Marshal Carter was not also involved. Maybe Larry would know. And maybe Larry would tell the truth about it. Or not.

"Shit!" Longarm complained aloud to the night birds and the cicadas.

He put the bay into a lope down the road toward where he had left the wagons.

Chapter 31

Longarm reined the bay to a halt atop a small rise some-where in the vast grasslands of Wyoming Territory. Macklin was a day and a half behind them.

The weight of the sun was heavy on his chest. His thoughts were much heavier.

For a man who liked the Big Empty, the scene before him was beautiful. A pair of hunting hawks circled effort-lessly on the sun-warmed rising air. A small herd of prong-horn antelope lay on a hillside, at rest but alert to all that was around them. The day was a picture of tranquillity. But for a man who was searching for two kidnapped women . . .

Longarm stepped down from the saddle, removed his coat and carefully folded it, then tied it down behind the cantle of his borrowed saddle. Petey nudged the pinto up close, the burro trailing placidly behind him.

"Are we lost, sir?"

"No, son, we ain't lost. But I got t' tell you that I've lost the trail. It isn't easy tracking something over buffalo grass sod like this is, but I'd've thought I'd find *some* mark of their passage. What I'm beginning t' think, boy, is that they've turned in a different direction. North maybe. They could be headed for the gold diggings up in Lead or maybe in Deadwood."

Petey looked worried. "My mama . . ."

"I know, boy. I ain't giving up on her. D'you need to get down for a minute? T' take a leak or anything?"

The boy shook his head. "I'm fine, thanks."

Longarm smiled. "Kid, you got the biggest bladder in you that I ever knowed of. Bigger'n mine, that's for sure." He turned around, unbuttoned and took a satisfying piss, then put himself back in order and once again stepped into the McClellan. "Let's go."

An hour later, they topped a rise and looked down into a shallow valley that appeared to be carpeted. Carpeted with wool. And the wool was still on the sheep. There must have been upward of two thousand of the creatures. They shifted and flowed as they grazed. And bleated, complaining about something. The noise coming from the flock was muted but nearly constant, more like a continuing buzz than individual voices. But then there was little of the individual in a flock of sheep.

Longarm pointed. "Can you see, Petey? On the hillside over there."

"I don't . . . oh, that." A dark spot on the grass jumped up and began running, charging at an escaping member of the flock and barking furiously until it forced the sheep back into the group. "It's a dog, isn't it? Wow! I heard about sheep dogs but I never seen one do anything like that."

"They're something special," Longarm said. "I'll confess it. I like t' see them work."

"Isn't there any people with them?"

"Of course. Look there." Longarm's pointing finger swept around to the right.

"All right. I see it now." Petey laughed. "It's a little house."

"Sort of, but this little house has wheels under it. It's really just a good, rugged wagon with a little house built onto

122

it instead of the canvas wagon covers like you're used to seeing. I tell you what, kid. We'll go over there an' see can we take our dinner with the sheepherder. If we act nice, maybe he'll let you look inside his caravan."

"Caravan?"

"That's what they call those things. Damned if I know why."

"Do you really think I could look?"

"That ain't up to me, but I'd think maybe." Longarm had more reason than a meal for wanting to visit with the sheepherder. It had been too damned long since he had seen any sign of the kidnappers. Maybe the sheep tender had seen them. "Come on, Petey. Let's go see the man."

Chapter 32

"I am Sebastian Moore, and I am a drunkard, sir. A drunk and a blight upon the human race." A huge grin split his seamed and leathery face. "I explain that to everyone, sir. It saves time. I am, however, sober now and doing penance for all my sins."

Longarm introduced himself and Petey and said, "We saw your caravan an' thought t' drop by, maybe ask for your help."

"I would be honored, sir." The smile widened. "And pleasured as well."

"We have coffee an' bacon enough t' share. Perhaps we could use your fire, Mr. Moore?"

"Of course. Anything. My humble camp is yours to use however you wish."

Longarm picked up his stirrup and flung it over the seat of his McClellan so he could get to the cinches. He loosened them and tied the bay on Moore's short hitch line where a pair of very heavy-bodied Clydesdales already were quietly standing. Then he went back to help Petey lift their packs down from the burro. The boy already had his own saddle loose and was working on the cinches for the packsaddle. The kid was definitely a help around camp.

Longarm rummaged through their supplies for the makings of a lunch, then added a treat that he thought Sebastian Moore might enjoy, a fresh apple. And yes, he did want to butter the man up a little.

"How the hell did you find an apple at this time of year? And it isn't even wrinkled like it would be if it came out of a root cellar storing last year's crop." Moore dipped water into a battered and soot-blackened old coffeepot, then dumped in a handful of fresh grounds.

"The way I understand it," Longarm said, hunkering down beside the sheepherder's fire, "is that these apples was growed all the way down in South America someplace, Chile I b'lieve the man said, and brought up here on a steamer, sold to a broker in San Francisco, an' shipped east by rail. Tasty things. I figure you got plenty o' canned fruit . . . an' there's nothing wrong with that . . . but it's likely been a spell since you seen a fresh apple."

"If you don't mind then, I will put it aside and have it after my supper tonight. Something that special deserves the proper timing so I can savor the experience as well as the taste."

"Whatever you want, friend."

Petey followed close on Moore's footsteps when he walked over to his caravan. When Moore opened the door on the back of the narrow wagon, Petey was still behind him, trying to peep around past his hip so he could see inside.

"Curious about how I live, eh? Well, go ahead then. Go in an' look around all you like."

"Really? Thanks, mister." The boy did not wait for Moore to change his mind. He scampered up the steps and inside the cramped quarters. Moore returned to the fire, leaving Petey to marvel and gawk however much he pleased.

"While the boy is in there," Longarm said, "mayhap I should explain t' you who he is an' why I'm on the prowl with a ten-year-old boy for a sidekick."

"After more than two months without hearing the sound of another human voice," Sebastian Moore said, "I can assure you I will be interested in whatever you have to tell me."

Longarm explained about the murder and the kidnappings. "The boy is the one can identify the men. Maybe the horses too. An' o' course his mother an' sister. The problem now is that we've lost their trail an' ain't entirely sure which way they're headed. North toward Deadwood maybe, but that ain't for sure."

"I believe I may have seen them," Moore said. He pursed his lips and reached for a plug of tobacco. He bit off a healthy chew, offered the twist to Longarm, and when it was declined returned it to his pocket. "The day before yesterday I saw a party of four men and . . ." He shook his head. "But there was only one woman in this group, not two."

"You're sure o' that?"

Moore nodded. "They never approached my camp, in fact they shied away from it and rode wide around me, but I have a good spyglass in there"— he nodded in the direction of his caravan—"and I looked them over. You see, one or two traveling past usually mean no harm, but any time there is a large group, there is the possibility they could be cattlemen, the sort who hate sheep and try to kill them. Or kill the herder." Sebastian smiled. "I also have a rifle, you see, and am not so easy to kill."

"You ain't doing nothing wrong if you defend yourself," Longarm said.

"Anyway, sir, about the party that passed here the day before yesterday, I am quite sure there were four adult males and one grown woman. They may not have been the people you are looking for."

Longarm glanced toward the caravan, then lowered his voice. "What I'm fretful about is that they *could* be the kidnappers."

"But with only one . . ." Moore paused, then frowned. "Oh, I . . . see what you mean. That poor child."

"Yeah. I agree."

"This coffee seems to be ready. Let me give it a moment for the grounds to settle, then we shall try it, eh?"

Longarm went to their packs and brought out a cup. Coffee sounded pretty good. Of course a drink and a woman would have been even better, but neither of those was to be. The coffee and a bite to eat would just have to do for now.

Chapter 33

More than likely, Longarm calculated as he and Petey rode along, if the kidnappers had disposed of one captive, it would have been the kid's mother. The sister was young and pretty and full of sass. According to her brother, the girl had had more than her share of suitors. The kidnappers likely enjoyed having her to pass around of an evening just like they might pass a bottle around or a pouch of tobacco.

But an older woman like Mrs. Sanderson would be a drain on both their resources and their patience. She could cook, but anyone could do that. She could fuck, but they had the young and pretty daughter for that.

No, Longarm figured, if one of the women was dead or abandoned—more likely dead than turned loose to tell her story—it was almost certainly the mother who lay somewhere back there in an unmarked grave.

This was not turning out to be a good trip for young Peter.

Longarm was careful to keep his thoughts from Petey, though. He only hoped that when the truth was given to him, it would be by his sister so he would have a loving family member to hold him and cry with him.

"D'you see that cabin down there beside those trees, boy?"

129

"Yes, sir."

"If I remember a'right, there's a creek down there an' a cabin beside a crossing."

"You've been here before?"

"Ayuh, I have. Last time I came through, that cabin was a trading post manned by a fella named Billy Wisdom." Longarm smiled. "Leastways, that's what he calls himself. God knows what his name used t' be. I'm gonna ride down an' talk with the gentleman. I want you t' keep on going"— he pointed—"across the creek an' between those hills. I'll catch up with you after I see Wisdom."

"Can't I come with you? Please?"

Longarm shook his head. "You ain't scared, are you?" Hell, yes, the kid would be scared to be riding off on his own. Of course he would. But there was no youngster on earth who would come right out and *admit* to such a thing when asked the direct question.

"No, sir, I'm not scared."

"Good. Now do what I say, please. I won't be long."

The truth was that Wisdom's post, assuming it hadn't changed in the past year or so, was probably what the term "den of iniquity" had been invented for. The only two commodities a man could buy there were whiskey and women. Longarm didn't think Wisdom's nasty little nest of vipers was the sort of place Petey should see.

On the other hand, it was *exactly* the sort of place a band of kidnappers and murderers would head for. It could even be the reason the Sanderson kidnappers chose to come this way.

It was unlikely that they would stay long, since they had their own female slave along to keep their gonads drained, but the whiskey would be attractive.

And with any kind of luck, the bastards would have stayed a little while to do their drinking instead of buying a jug and moving on. That would let Longarm and Petey catch up to them just that much quicker.

130

"Between those hills, sir?"

"That's right. But don't worry. I won't be long behind you."

"All right, sir."

Longarm stayed with the boy all the way down to the creek and saw the kid safely across, then turned the bay's head upstream toward Billy Wisdom's hog ranch.

Wisdom sold the worst kind of vile Injun whiskey, raw alcohol fortified with gunpowder and rattlesnake heads, or so the comments went.

But after the first couple drinks, the shit commenced to taste pretty good.

Longarm was looking forward to that as well as to whatever information Wisdom could give him.

He put the bay into an easy lope.

Chapter 34

Longarm tied the bay to the hitching rail—surprisingly sturdy even though the cabin it stood near looked like it was about to fall down—but left the cinches snug. At a place like Billy Wisdom's, a gent never knew when he might want to leave in too much of a hurry to be messing about with cinch straps.

Half a dozen other horses already tied at a rail, or hobbled and turned loose to browse, attested to the popularity of Wisdom's rotgut.

Longarm removed his coat, carefully folded it and tied it behind the cantle of his saddle, then took the several long strides necessary to reach the low doorway. He had to bend his knees and duck just a little to make it through to the interior of the place, and once inside he had to stop where he was for a long moment before his eyes could adjust to the sudden loss of light.

That, Longarm was sure, was a deliberately planned feature of the place, intended to take away any advantage of surprise should anyone come gunning for a patron.

Even before his eyes adjusted, Longarm was reminded of where he was. The scents of liquor, tobacco, and sour sweat were thick, but the buzz of conversations abruptly ended, chopped into total silence while the patrons looked him over. After a few seconds, the muted talk resumed. There must be no one in the place, he judged, who was wanted for anything.

There was not all that much worth looking at even after he could see clearly again. A gaggle of very poor-quality whores, mostly Indian women, occupied one end of the place. Some upended barrels with three-legged stools placed around them served as tables—hard to break and easy to replace if they did get shattered—while more empty beer barrels supported the wide planks that made up the bar.

A trio of customers stood at one end of the bar, hunched over drinks and busy with their own conversation. Two solitary drinkers stood nearby, and one man was asleep or passed out at one of the barrel-top tables.

Billy Wisdom was perched on his stool behind the bar. Wisdom could have been mistaken for another of the barrels he used for furniture. He certainly was shaped like one. The man had rolls of fat hanging under his chin, and he looked like he might not have gotten around to taking this year's bath quite yet.

In spite of Wisdom's bulk, Longarm knew, he was quick to grab up a bung starter and knock a man cross-eyed if need be, and he was almost as fast as Longarm when it came to using the Ivor Johnson .38 he carried in a shoulder rig. Longarm had seen Wisdom in action once and been amazed at the man's speed. The gent Wisdom shot at was more than impressed; he was dead.

Wisdom nodded when he saw Longarm and said, "Howdy, Custis. Care for a drink?"

"You know I would, thanks." Longarm found it interesting that Wisdom had not chosen to call him by his usual nickname, but greeted him as Custis instead. There was bound to be a reason for that. Longarm's name was certainly well known among a certain set, and probably one

134

of the customers would react badly to the idea that a law-man might be here asking questions. Worse for Wisdom if people got the idea that he would answer those questions. Longarm took the hint and stepped to the bar.

"How you doin', Billy?" Longarm asked, one elbow on the bar and an unlit cheroot between his teeth.

"Business is slow, but I get along." Wisdom scratched a match aflame and held it so Longarm could get a light from it.

"Thanks." Lordy, that first puff always tasted grand.

Wisdom set a mug in front of him and poured it half full of something—God knows what—from a bottle that might have been refilled a hundred times since it was new.

"Here's to you, Billy." Longarm lifted the mug and tried to sniff the contents. The alcohol was too raw and volatile to be smelled like that. Not if a man wanted to keep his nasal passages intact. Longarm rolled his eyes, held his breath, and took a swallow.

The alcohol burned like a sonuvabitch, and he was sure it was going to take the skin off his tongue. Or already had.

It tasted like thistles that had been marinating in horse piss. Come to think of it, maybe it was.

But it had fire in it when it hit his belly, and no one else in the room was dead from drinking it—yet—so it must be all right.

"That tastes good," Longarm wheezed, his eyes watering and his lips numb.

"You're a lying son of a bitch, Custis." Wisdom laughed. "But thank you for that endorsement."

Longarm smiled and knocked back the rest of his drink. Experience had taught him that seconds would be bearable and a third drink would taste like it came direct from the angels.

Billy Wisdom knew. He poured a refill without being asked.

"We can talk shortly," Wisdom said, "soon as my head

135

girl gets done with what she's doing. We'll step outside to where we can have some privacy."

"Fine," Longarm said. He downed the second drink, shuddered, and then smiled. The fire in his gut had turned to a mellow warmth now, and the whiskey was commencing to taste as smooth as nectar.

"Once more," he said, and Billy Wisdom poured again.

Chapter 35

"Ah, now that's fine," Longarm said, savoring the flavor of Billy Wisdom's liquor. He took another small drink and enjoyed the sense of warmth in his belly. "Just fine."

Wisdom was distracted by the rattle of fly beads as someone entered through the back door. That one led outside to a row of cribs where Billy's girls plied their trade.

Immediately on the heels of the fly beads came the sharp, lilac scent of cheap perfume. Longarm turned to see a woman who was younger and prettier than the usual run of Billy's women. This one had henna-red hair and tits as big as milk buckets. Which, come to think of it, they were.

Her rouge was smudged and her hair mussed, and she looked like she had been ridden hard and put away wet.

Just behind her came a lean, dark man who wore his pistols in a pair slung low on his hips. Just like Longarm had a few minutes earlier, he had to pause for a few seconds while his eyes adjusted to the dim light inside the saloon.

"You ought t' have a go at this one, Terry," he said loudly. "She's a good fuck. Pumps her ass real nice, little Cindy does."

"Maybe later," one of the gents at the bar said. "I ain't drunk enough yet."

When the first man could see again, his eyes went wide and his jaw dropped. "Long!" he bellowed. *"You son of a bitch!"*

He reached for both his guns at once. Perhaps he might have done better if he had practiced getting one revolver out at a time—but in a hurry—instead of being fancy about it. As it was, all he accomplished was to be slow on the draw.

Longarm reacted without taking time to think about it. His eyes recorded the message. His hand moved. No conscious thought was involved in the process.

His Colt came out and he pointed instinctively at the man's gut, at the same time dropping into a crouch.

The flat, hammering roar of Longarm's .45 filled the low-ceilinged saloon, and a cloud of white gun smoke billowed out from his muzzle.

The lean man who had just been with the painted whore coughed and looked down at his chest, where a splash of bright blood was beginning to stain the front of his shirt.

"Damn . . . damn you." He tried to raise his pistols, but of a sudden they seemed too heavy a burden to carry. "Damn you," he managed one more time. Then he sank to his knees and slowly toppled forward into the sawdust and the spit that covered Wisdom's floor.

Longarm took a step toward the dying man, but froze in place at the ominous *cla-clack* sound of a pistol being cocked behind his back, somewhere down the bar.

He was about to make a try for whoever that was, probably the first man's partner, but Billy Wisdom beat him to it. Wisdom's .38 barked. By the time Longarm turned around, it was over. The man who had tried to backshoot him was already dead with a .38 slug scrambling his brain.

The fellow hit the floor. His pistol discharged harmlessly into the sawdust and he joined his partner there.

Longarm quickly surveyed the room, but no one else was interested in joining the scrap. The man who was passed out on one of the tables hadn't even awakened.

"Thanks," Longarm said to Wisdom. His ears were ringing but—he checked—no damage had been done to his person. No bullets had come close.

Eyes still on the room, he thumbed a fresh cartridge out of his belt loops, flicked the loading gate of his Colt open, and swiftly reloaded.

Not that he expected to need it.

But then he had not expected to be shot at to begin with either.

"Can I ask you something, Billy?"

"Go ahead."

"Who the hell were those guys?"

Wisdom shrugged. "Beats me. I never saw them before." Which might or might not have been true, but whatever the truth, Longarm was pleased that Wisdom had not wanted the trouble that would have come down on him had a federal peace officer been murdered in his establishment.

Longarm tossed back the rest of the drink that he had left on the bar. "Come on. Let's have us that talk, you an' me, then I got t' get going. Got somebody waiting on me."

Billy Wisdom too reloaded his revolver. Then he rather ponderously climbed down off the stool where he reigned over his domain, and led the way out from behind his bar and through the back door.

Longarm had to bend low to make it through. Billy Wisdom walked beneath the lintel without ducking and without coming close to bumping his head.

The whore who had just been with the dead cowboy slipped in behind the bar to take care of things until the boss got back.

Chapter 36

"Four men," Longarm said, "traveling with two women . . . maybe just one. They would've been through here day before yesterday or thereabouts."

Wisdom nodded. "I know them. Alva White, Chuck Hill, Raymond Danaher, and Barney something. I never heard his last name. If he ever had one. He's a sonuvabitch, that one." Wisdom looked around for something to sit on, found a discarded crate lying amid the litter behind his saloon, upended it, and sat on that. "They were here yesterday."

That was encouraging, Longarm thought. They were getting closer to the kidnappers again after having been thrown off the trail for a while there. "Were there any women with them?"

The fat saloonkeeper shook his head. "Not that I saw. Which doesn't mean they didn't have some staked out in the trees waiting for them while they came in for their liquor."

"What did they do, Billy? How did they act?"

"They acted normal enough, I suppose. Seemed like they were in a bit of a hurry, but not like anybody was chasing them. Alva, Chuck, and Ray came in and bought a drink apiece, then one more. I recall that a fellow at one of the tables there was looking to get a card game together.

He invited them to join in, but they weren't interested. Said they had a schedule to keep. If you can believe that. Then they left, and practically on their heels Barney came in. He tossed back a short one, then paid for two jugs of whiskey that he carried out with him. I know they were all together because Barney paid for everything, including the drinks the first ones had."

"Did they say anything about where they might be going?"

"Let me think." Wisdom looked away, his eyes unfocused as he tried to remember customers from a full day before.

Longarm took out a cheroot and fiddled with it, taking his time about nipping the twist off and lighting the little cigar, wanting to be patient and give Billy all the time he needed to think back over what the kidnappers might have said within his hearing.

After a minute or so, Wisdom's gaze returned to Longarm. "What I said about keeping a schedule? Well, what they actually said, I think, was something about 'a stage to catch.'"

Longarm frowned. A stagecoach to meet? Where? Why? That did not seem to make much sense.

No, not to meet. To catch. Was the distinction important? Dammit, he wished he knew more. If he just knew where they were going, he could try to get ahead of them or at least move fast and not have to track them. Tracking was necessarily a slow and exacting process.

"Did they say anything else? Where they were going, for instance?"

Wisdom shook his head. Then he snapped his fingers and said, "No, wait, I do remember something more, Longarm. I asked one of them . . . Alva, I think . . . if they were on their way to Deadwood. He said no, they were going to a dance." Wisdom frowned and thought for a moment more. "Come to think of it now, he said they were going to 'the' dance."

"Do you know of anyone holding a dance in this country, Billy?"

"Not a peep, and believe me, if anyone was hosting a big dance, I would hear about it from the cowboys who visit my place. Cowboys like gatherings like that. They'll ride half a week to get to one. The last dance I heard about, though, was more than a month ago at Gerald Rick's ranch over on Crazy Woman Creek."

"Going to the dance," Longarm repeated. Then he shrugged. "All right. Thanks, Billy. I owe you one."

The saloon keeper grunted and said, "Damn right you do, Longarm. I'll collect on that debt one of these days. Count on it."

"Fair is fair, Billy. And by the way. Thanks for saving my bacon in there."

"Oh, you would have gotten him without me," Wisdom said. "Besides, I can't abide a backshooter. I never interfere if someone wants to fight face-to-face, but I won't allow any backshooting." He smiled. "Something like that would give the place a bad name."

"Maybe, but . . . thank you."

"Any time."

Longarm asked, "Do you need a hand with those bodies?"

"Thanks, but I can handle it. If, uh, if there is a bounty on either of them? . . ."

"It's yours," Longarm said. He had no intention of hanging around here trying to determine who the dead men were or if there was paper out on them. Wisdom was more than welcome to the bounty if there was one.

Both men glanced toward the doorway when two people emerged, but it was only a cowhand squiring a short Mexican whore toward one of the cribs. The girl was not especially pretty, but she was young and had enormous tits.

Longarm waited until those two disappeared, then said, "Billy, thanks. For everything."

143

Wisdom nodded and struggled onto his feet before heading back into his saloon.

Longarm took another drag on his cheroot, then walked around the side of the building, stopped to take a piss against the wall, and on around to where he had left the bay.

Going to the dance.

What fucking dance? Where?

Chapter 37

He forded the creek, then stopped at the edge of the wooded fringe to survey the country ahead. A man never knew where danger might wait, and caution was simple common sense out here.

Back East, or so he was given to understand, a man could walk the streets in near-perfect safety and many men did not so much as own a gun, much less go about their daily affairs carrying one.

Custis Long had never known a day during which his life might not be forfeit. His boyhood was marked by feuding in his native West Virginia, and as a young man he was caught up in the boredom punctuated by terror and gun smoke that was war.

He hoped young Petey would have a less threatening existence. Starting just as soon as Longarm could find those kidnappers.

Once out on the open grass, he put the spurs to the bay and the sleek animal broke into a rocking-chair canter, the horse's long strides eating up ground. Within fifteen or twenty minutes, he could see the boy and the burro moving steadily forward, just as Longarm had told him to do. Petey was a good kid. Longarm just hoped the boy was not an orphan.

"Were you getting worried?" he asked once he caught up with the boy.

Petey grinned. "No, sir. You said you'd come. I knew you would. Did you find out anything back there?"

"A little." Longarm told him the men's names. "I found out they bought some whiskey. No surprise there. Didn't learn where they're bound, though, or what their intentions might be." Scowling, he added, "They said somethin' about going to 'the dance.' Whatever the hell that means. The dance. Like as if that's supposed t' mean something an' not just to them. 'The dance.'" He shook his head, annoyed with himself for not being able to puzzle out the meaning of those two words. "Sorry, kid. I'd hoped for more'n that."

"You know their names. You can put out posters on them. If we don't catch them. If . . . you know."

If his mother and sister were dead. The unspoken fear was in his eyes. Longarm said, "We'll do our best, Petey. If you do that in your life, son, you won't have cause for regret. Just do your very best."

"Yes, sir." After a few minutes of riding in silence, Petey gigged his pinto forward beside the bay, the burro trotting docilely along beside him. "This evening when we stop for supper, sir, can I practice some with my rifle? Do we have enough ammunition that I can use some?"

Longarm thought he understood what the boy was thinking. He nodded. "Sure. Quick as we get a fire started an' the animals tended. You know where the .22 cartridges are." He smiled. "If there's time, I'll let you try a few rounds with my .45 too. Just so you know how it feels."

The boy's eyes went wide and his grin was even bigger. "Thank you, sir."

Longarm shook his head. "Kid, I just don't know how I'm ever gonna break you of calling me 'sir.'" But the truth was that he had come to sort of like it.

Hours later, Longarm lay sleeping by the faint light of

a dwindling fire in which little more than coals and ash remained.

He came awake with a start and sat bold upright, his eyes suddenly as wide open as the boy's had been that afternoon.

"Of course," he muttered into the silence of the breeze moving across the prairie. "The dance. O' course."

Then, chuckling softly, he lay back down and quickly drifted into a deep and untroubled sleep.

Tomorrow early they would head for the dance.

Chapter 38

Once they were freed from the necessity of looking for tracks, Longarm was able to go hell-for-leather toward "the dance" where the kidnappers were headed.

Or . . . *almost* hell-for-leather.

"Kid, I got bad news for you. We need t' put some miles behind us, an' that little burro won't be able t' keep up. I figure the best thing t' do is t' just strip packs an' stuff off him an' turn him loose. He'll have grass an' water out here, and more'n likely he'll turn up in somebody's ranch yard by and by."

"But . . . he's my friend, sir."

"I know that, but we got t' be moving right along."

The boy's eyes welled up with tears, but he set his jaw and did not say anything further. When they saddled the bay and the pinto, the burro's pack and gear remained where they were.

Slowly, sadly, the child unfastened the lead rope from the little burro's halter. Without a word, but with tears running down his face and dripping from his chin, he gave the burro a hug and rubbed its fuzzy ears, then crawled onto the saddle of his pinto. He took up his reins and sat waiting for Longarm to lead the way.

"Aw, *shit*!" Longarm grumbled. The burro was only a damned work animal. A tool, dammit. That was all.

And yet . . .

His friend, the kid said. Lord knows he had few enough of those now. His pa was dead and torn apart by coyotes. His mother and sister might well be dead too. At least one of them almost certainly was, judging by what that sheepherder said he saw from a distance.

Now the boy was being told to abandon the only comfort he had left in this life.

"Shit," Longarm repeated.

He clipped the lead rope back onto the halter and led the burro to its usual spot trailing the pinto. Handing the lead rope to Petey, he said, "We'll do our best t' see if he can keep up. All right?"

Peter sniffled a little and wiped the back of his hand under his nose. He nodded. "Yes, sir."

"I ain't promising nothing," Longarm swore. "But we'll see."

"Yes, sir."

Promise or no, dammit, he knew good and well they were not going to cast the burro loose. The little bastard was going with them to the dance at whatever his best speed proved to be.

Longarm swung onto the bay and led off at a brisk walk long enough to let the animals warm up. Then he put the horse into a lope, checking over his shoulder every so often until he was satisfied that the burro could keep up.

After a while he quit fretting about it. Petey and the burro kept up with him better than he expected.

Two days later, late in the afternoon, Longarm brought the bay to a halt and motioned for the boy to come alongside.

"We aren't stopping for supper this early, are we?" the kid asked.

Longarm shook his head and pointed. "You see that hill? Mountain some call it. Right over there."

"Yes, sir, of course."

"Well, that mountain is sacred to the Sioux. Other tribes too. I disremember the name they call it by, but us whites have come to call it Sundance Mountain. That's because the Sioux come there t' hold their ceremonial sun dances.

"There's a pole up on top o' that mountain, an' the Indians tie leather ropes to the top o' the pole. The fasten the other ends o' those ropes to pegs. Know where they put the pegs? Right through the skin on the chests of whatever warrior claims he's had a vision about it. Then the warriors dance around the pole an' try to tear themselves free. Sometimes they dance for hours an' fling themselves against the ropes.

"If you meet an Indian warrior an' he has sort of H-shaped scars on his chest right here an' here"—Longarm touched himself above each nipple—"that shows he's done the sun dance. It means he has power in the tribe. Not the kind of power we think of, but a sort of magical power. It means something right special to an Indian, so if you see it be respectful of it. That Indian has earned respect among his own kind, an' you should give it too."

"Yes, sir."

"How's your burro holding up?"

Petey grinned. "He's fine, sir. Just fine."

"That's good because he's made it all the way. Right over there."—Longarm pointed again, this time just to the west of Sundance Mountain—"is where we're going. There ain't much of a town there, or wasn't the last time I was up this way, but there's folks and some has come to call it 'the dance,' so I figure this is where those kidnappers are headed. With any kind of luck, we've either got here

151

ahead o' them or they're still here, but I figure this is a good shot at catchin' them. Come along, boy. Let's see what we can find at the dance."

Longarm nudged the bay into a trot. Petey and the burro trailed faithfully behind.

Chapter 39

There just was not a whole hell of a lot to the rough little village of Sundance. A small clutch of stores. A scattering of houses. And that was about it.

"Why are we here, sir?"

"Damned if I know, Petey, but if the kidnappers are headed this way, they know. Truth be told, you and me don't need t' know why they come here. All we got t' do is to find them."

Longarm led his little cavalcade onto the main street of Sundance, his eyes without conscious thought inspecting the horses he saw tied there. He did not see any that resembled what he had been told about the kidnappers' mounts. That could have been a good thing; they had not yet reached "the dance." Or bad; they had been here and gone.

"Let's see if we can stay at that house over there," he said, pointing with his chin to a small place on the southeast edge of the community.

"There's a hotel over there, sir."

"I know that, but from the porch o' that house a body can see anything headed into town."

"But, sir, there's no sign saying they take in boarders. What if? . . ."

Longarm smiled. "Kid, trust me here. We are gonna go talk to whoever lives in that house, and I am gonna tell some whoppers. Not lies exactly, but . . . well, all right, they'll be out-an'-out lies. Which I ordinarily don't like t' do. But you'll understand later on."

"All right, sir. I'll be quiet whatever you say."

"Good. Now let's go talk to whoever owns the place."

There was no hitch rail outside the house, and he knew he would not endear himself to the homeowner by tying their animals to the purely decorative little white picket fence that fronted the place, so he took the time to hobble the horses rather than trust them to ground-tie. The burro was allowed to roam free. The fuzzy-eared creature would not wander far from the horses.

"Leave your rifle here, Petey. Lean it up against the fence. I wouldn't want you t' give the wrong impression when we get up onto that porch."

"Somebody could take it, sir."

"See anybody walkin' around close here? No? Your gun will be fine. I promise."

"Yes, sir."

Longarm paused for a moment to lift his Stetson and use the heel of his hand to smooth his hair back. Then he opened the spring-loaded gate and led the way onto the front porch of the house where he wanted to stay. His knock was answered by a tall, severe woman in a linen apron who held a feather duster in one hand.

The woman had auburn hair that was beginning to go gray. She had sharply angular features. The sort that looked like a man could use her face to chop wood. Her nose was long and pointed, her chin chiseled out of solid granite. Her eyes were hooded and dark. Most prominent, though, was a dark red birthmark that covered most of the left side of her face. She made no attempt to hide it, but looked down her nose as if daring this stranger to comment on the disfigurement.

"May I ask what you want here?" Her voice was as sharp as the planes of her face. It was *not* welcoming.

"Sorry t' bother you, ma'am," Longarm said, snatching his hat off and holding it in front of his belly . . . where it rather conveniently covered the butt of the Colt revolver he carried there.

He introduced himself to the lady and then reached back and put a hand on Petey's shoulder.

"The boy and me need t' stay here a few days, an' I think it'd be an awful shame to be leaving him alone in some hotel room while I go about my business here. There's no telling the low sort of men he'd be exposed to there. Gambling too and all manner of rowdiness. The boy is an orphan, y'see, and I'm responsible for him." Petey gave Longarm a slightly startled look when he said that. "What I was hoping was t' find a decent home . . . like yours, ma'am . . . where we could take a room for just a day or two." That should give the kidnappers time to get here, he figured.

"Who told you that you could board here?"

"Nobody, ma'am. We just now rode in from down south. Haven't even found a place to board our animals yet nor spoken to another human person before you."

The woman scowled.

"Please, ma'am?" Petey put in, opening his mouth for the first time.

"We'd pay, o' course," Longarm said. "I'm here on official business, so the gov'ment would be good for reasonable charges for room an' board. Or just for a room if you don't want t' bother with feedin' us."

The woman appeared to be wavering.

"He's a good boy, ma'am, an' quiet."

"You are not a smoker, are you?" the woman asked.

"I am, ma'am, I admit it. But I could do it out here on your porch. I wouldn't have t' bring any smoke inside your fine home."

"Mr. Long, you are being blatantly flattering. You haven't seen inside my home to call it fine."

"I have every confidence that it is, ma'am." Longarm grinned.

"Never trust a flatterer, the old saying goes."

"Never trust an old saying when there's two tired travelers that's in need of a meal an' a bed," Longarm countered.

For the first time a smile creased that craggy, marred, and in truth quite ugly face. "I do believe you are a rapscallion, Mr. Long."

"I been called worse, but never by anybody nicer."

"Flatterer indeed. All right. A dollar a night for the two of you. That includes board. I have nowhere to put the animals, however."

"We'll find a place for them, ma'am. Just let us bring our saddlebags inside while you show us to our room. Then we'll go on into town an' take care o' the horses. Maybe look around a little bit before we come back in time for supper." He frowned. "Come to think of it, you didn't know you'd have people in, an' likely aren't prepared t' feed two hungry travelers. Is there a place in town where we can get our supper before we settle in for the evening?"

"That is very thoughtful of you, Mr. Long. Come inside then. I have separate rooms for you. You needn't bed down together."

"So much the better, ma'am."

"And my name is Judith Ledbetter, Mr. Long. Just so you know."

"My pleasure, Miz Ledbetter."

"Thank you, ma'am. Thanks a lot," Petey put in. He turned and ran back to drag both pairs of saddlebags off the bay and the pinto.

Chapter 40

Judith Ledbetter speared Petey's .22 with a disapproving eye when he carried it inside her house.

Longarm leaned close and whispered, "It's his first rifle, ma'am. The boy even sleeps with it."

Mrs. Ledbetter sniffed loudly. But she did not order Petey to remove the offensive article from her home.

She showed them to a pair of tiny bedrooms at the back of the place, rooms probably intended for servants, but now vacant except for beds with bare mattresses and a washstand and basin in each room.

Longarm let Petey have his choice between them, then deposited his dusty saddlebags on the floor beside the washstand.

"You said you will eat elsewhere tonight?"

"Yes, ma'am, I expect we should. An' we got to get the animals settled someplace too."

She gave them directions to the feed store, which doubled as a livery in Sundance, and recommended a café. "While you are there, I can tend to those rooms. They need dusting. Sheets, blankets. Do you like to sleep with a pillow?"

"Yes, ma'am. That's a real treat," Petey said.

"I shall see you have some. And water. You will need

water in your rooms to wash and to shave." She looked at Petey. "I suppose you prefer hot water for shaving." She said it with a deadpan expression that nearly made Longarm break up laughing.

"Oh, I don't shave, ma'am. Yet," Petey said, as serious as could be. Longarm practically had to stuff a fist down his throat to keep from ruining the lady's moment.

Longarm and the boy left their gear in the rooms and walked back toward the front of the house. "What time d'you lock your doors at night, ma'am?" Longarm asked.

She gave him an odd look, then said, "I don't. We have no problems with thievery here. I never lock my doors. Why, I am not exactly sure where the key is should I wish to lock it."

"That's the sign of a mighty fine town," Longarm said. He turned to Petey. "Come along, boy. There's things we need t' do. Then we'll have us some supper."

"Yes, sir." Petey scampered out to the front porch. Then the boy stuck his head back inside and shouted, "Thank you, ma'am." A faint "You're welcome" came from somewhere in the back of the house where Mrs. Ledbetter was making up the beds for her two new boarders.

Longarm swung into the saddle of his bay and Petey climbed onto the pinto, lead rope in hand. They walked a hundred fifty yards or so to the feed barn and talked to a man in the office there.

"Aye, I'll board your horses. Quarter a day each."

"What about the burro?"

"What about him?"

"I mean what's the charge to board him?"

"I just told you. Twenty-five cents. Seventy-five-cent total for the three head."

"That seems mighty dear for such a little thing. He couldn't eat much," Longarm said.

"Then I'll make a better profit off him, won't I?" the feed man countered. His chin came up belligerently and he demanded, "Well? What'll it be? You gonna leave them here or ain't you?"

"We'll leave them."

"Good. Seventy-five cents. In advance." The man held his hand out. Longarm had an idea what he would *like* to do with that hand. Instead, he minded his manners and paid out a dollar and a half to cover them for two nights.

"You can throw your kak over there," the feed man said, pointing. "Nobody will bother it." He turned and went back inside his office.

Longarm nudged Petey with his elbow. "Reckon we lucked out when we found Miz Ledbetter, eh?"

The boy grinned at him.

"Come along, kid. Let's you an' me go put on the feed bag."

Petey picked up his .22 and dropped it into the crook of his arm the way he had seen Longarm carry his Winchester.

Chapter 41

Sundance had no peace officers of its own, so there was no one Longarm needed to check in with. On the other hand, because there was no town marshal, there was no one he could turn to for local knowledge, and any man in town could be a friend of the kidnappers. At least initially, Longarm wanted to keep his mouth shut and his ears open.

After supper—plain but filling and not expensive—Longarm took Petey back to Mrs. Ledbetter's house and got him settled in for the night.

"I'm gonna go see if I can find a card game t' relax me before I go to bed," he told the boy. "You stay here. You need the outhouse or a drink of anything?"

"No, sir."

"All right then. I'll see you in the mornin'. Get a good sleep."

"Sir."

"Mm?"

"Could you . . . could you tuck me in . . . like my pa used to do? If you wouldn't mind, I mean."

"Sure. I can do that." Tucking kids into their beds at night was not something Longarm was well practiced at, but he managed. The simple task gave him a funny feeling.

161

Protective and sort of, well, sort of tender. Who the hell would have guessed? "Good night, Petey."

He let himself out and softly closed the bedroom door.

Judith Ledbetter was in her parlor reading when Longarm passed through the room on his way out. The light from her lamp was directed onto her book, leaving her face in deep shadow. The house was silent save for the tread of Longarm's footsteps.

The lady looked up from her reading and said, "I shall leave a lamp burning for you, Mr. Long. Please use it to light your way to bed, then blow it out. I can collect it from your room tomorrow."

"Yes, ma'am." He touched the brim of his Stetson. "Good night, ma'am."

"Good night, Mr. Long." Even her voice was spare and as hard as iron. Longarm wondered if the woman was capable of bending. He rather doubted it. She seemed completely rigid and severe.

He led himself out into the cool or the evening and stopped on the porch to light a cheroot. For a minute or so he just stood there, taking in the air and enjoying the flavor of his cigar and the feel of the breeze. Then he headed down the street in search of a saloon where he could listen and perhaps learn.

Three hours later and four dollars poorer, but with no more information about the four kidnappers than he had had to begin with, Longarm went back to the Ledbetter house and let himself in.

Mrs. Ledbetter's book lay facedown in the seat of her reading chair. The lamp burned beside it, the wick turned down low. Longarm carried the lamp to his room and quickly undressed.

He stood beside the small bed wearing his underthings, and looked around for the usual thunder mug so he could take a leak before going to sleep. The evening's drinks were making themselves felt in his bladder and he definitely needed to piss.

Shit! There seemed to be no choice about it. He was going to have to go out again to relieve himself.

There was no sign of Mrs. Ledbetter, so he assumed she was asleep. And he did not want to go through the bother of completely dressing again. He settled for stepping into his boots and slipping out again, leaving the lamp burning on the washstand beside his bed and the door open to allow a little of its light to spill out into the hallway and beyond to the kitchen.

He went out through the kitchen door and stood on the back porch. Rather than make the trek out to the backhouse, he relieved himself onto the low bushes that were growing beside the house, then tucked himself back in and returned to the kitchen.

In order to get to his room, he had to pass by Mrs. Ledbetter's bedroom. It had been dark when he went outside. The door was ajar but the room was dark. He was certain of that. Now . . .

A low light glowed yellow inside her room, inevitably drawing his attention in the otherwise dark and silent house.

Wondering if something was wrong, if there was an illness or something, Longarm silently moved closer and took a peek inside.

Mrs. Ledbetter was seated on the side of her bed, brushing her hair.

She did not have a lick of clothing on, not so much as a thread.

And she had one fine figure if a man liked them long and lean.

Longarm felt his dick grow hard at the sight of her. It had been a long time since he last was with a woman.

"Come in, Mr. Long. I have been waiting for you."

Longarm stepped into the lady's bedroom. He stood for a moment, looking at her and liking what he saw.

Then he turned and very carefully closed her bedroom door behind him. He made sure it was latched shut lest Petey pass by on his way to the backhouse.

He turned, smiling, and faced the lady of the house.

Chapter 42

Judith helped Longarm out of his clothing, rushing to pull offending cloth and leather out of her way. And she managed to do it while at the same time sticking her tongue halfway down his throat. At least that was what it felt like.

Within moments he was bare-ass naked, and the woman smiled at the size of him.

She took his hand and pulled him down onto the soft, feather mattress in her big bed. Her mouth covered his hungrily and her tongue never left his mouth until he was on the bed with her. Then she rolled onto her side and began licking his mouth, nose, into his ears.

He liked that, but felt vaguely discomforted by the way she was taking control of things.

Longarm pushed her off and rolled her onto her back. "Just a minute," he said.

He left the bed and stood. The lone lamp burned with a low flame. Longarm turned it up to give more light. He found a block of lucifers and lit the two other lamps in the room and turned them up too.

"So I can see you better," he explained.

Judith smiled.

He stood for a moment at her bedside, looking down at

what was offered. Judith Ledbetter had a fine body. Better than he would have expected from her stiff demeanor and attire. But then a dress can hide quite as much as it can enhance. Judith chose to hide what she had to offer even though it was plenty.

Her tits were firm, tipped with pale nipples that he guessed would be a good two fingers long or close to it. And so hard she could hang her hat on one.

Her belly was flat and her bush sparse over a very prominent pussy mound. She had long, slim legs and practically no hips.

Her hair was down now and brushed to a sheen.

Longarm was smiling when he rejoined her on the bed.

"Better?" she asked.

"Mm," he muttered while he nuzzled the side of her neck and licked her left ear.

He moved down to her tit and tasted of one of those long, skinny nipples. Judith moaned and arched her back to him. He felt the light play of her fingers in his hair on the back of his head, urging him to stay there a little longer. He was glad to oblige.

"Do you want me to suck your cock?" she whispered.

"In a minute." He smiled. "You can get me up for seconds."

"Seconds? My dear man, you haven't given me that lovely thing the first time yet."

"I can fix that."

Judith opened her legs to him and Longarm knelt there, probing with the head of his cock, then finding the opening he sought and sliding into a warm, tight passage that was already wet in anticipation of his entry.

"Lovely," Judith said as she lifted her hips to him.

Warmth turned to heat and she began pumping in rhythm with his thrusts. Slow at first. Then gathering in speed and intensity.

It took only seconds for the first exhilarating explosion

of his seed into her body. Longarm grunted and thrust as hard and as deep as he could. Trying to pierce her with the sword of his flesh. Trying to drive all the way through her.

Judith cried out aloud as she too reached a climax.

Longarm collapsed on top of her. Spent. At least for this moment, sated.

After a few seconds he moved, trying to take some of his weight onto his elbows so he would not be so heavy on her. He was lying almost completely on Judith's body and barely touching her mattress.

"No. Wait. I like having you on top of me. Still inside me. Stay there just a minute longer."

He could hear the smile in her voice when she added, "In a minute I will lick your juices away and suck you." She laughed. "You did promise me seconds, you know."

"Oh, I wouldn't forget a thing like that," he said. "But I like what I'm feelin' right now too. It's nice an' warm in there and it feels sort o' "—he laughed—"friendly."

"Yes," she agreed, "I believe you could say that this is a friendly thing to do."

His hard-on had barely subsided. Now it returned to full strength. He pulled it out of the heat of her body. Judith made a sad face at the loss. When the head slipped free and his cock was fully exposed, the air was chill on his wet dick, almost uncomfortably so.

But he knew the cure for that.

Longarm rolled onto his back and gave Judith a nudge. "Let's see how far down your throat you can take that thing, woman."

As it turned out, she could take it quite far.

Chapter 43

Longarm did not get much sleep that night, but in the morning he felt fit as a fiddle; he had gotten something much better than sleep.

He woke before the first rays of sunlight came streaming over the eastern horizon, but even so Judith was up ahead of him. He could hear her humming happily as she prepared breakfast for her boarders.

Petey, on the other hand, was not so easy to chase out of bed. The boy was enjoying being able to sleep in a real bed again after their days on the trail coming up from Nebraska.

"C'mon, kid. This might be the day we run up agin those kidnappers."

That brought him out from under the covers in a hurry. Petey slipped into his clothes while Longarm splashed some water into the basin for him.

"Don't forget t' wash behind your ears now."

"Yes, sir." The boy stopped in mid-wash, droplets of cold water dripping off his chin. "Do you think there is a real chance we might see them, sir?"

Longarm nodded. "I don't give you no guarantees, but I wouldn't think we could've got here very much ahead o' them. I'd guess them t' be somewhere around here if this is indeed where they was headed, an' if they follow their usual pattern, one or two o' them will come into town t' fetch supplies and see to whatever business it is that they got here."

Petey's expression hardened. He said nothing, but Longarm was fairly sure that he had a good idea what the boy was thinking. His mother, his sister . . . and his father dead and torn apart by coyotes . . . those four men had a lot to answer for.

"Finish up, son. If I'm hearin' right, Miz Ledbetter is puttin' our breakfast on the table right about now." He ruffled the boy's hair. "We wouldn't want it t' get cold."

"Yes, sir." Petey quickly dried his hands on his shirt and headed for the door. Longarm followed close behind him.

Judith laid a huge breakfast out for them. Longarm noticed that Petey was not so excited that he lost his appetite. It was difficult for a bachelor to remember just how much a growing boy could put into his belly. Even so, they finished their meal in short order and went out onto the porch on the pretext of working off the meal on the rocking chairs out there. In truth there was another reason, the one why Longarm had been so anxious to take rooms in this particular house.

From this porch they could get a good look at anyone riding in from the east or from the south.

"You're the only one of us has seen these sons o' bitches," Longarm reminded the boy, "so I'm counting on you t' keep an eagle eye out for anybody you recognize. If you see a familiar face, I want you t' let me know. No need t' shout, mind you. A nod or a touch on my sleeve will do. All you got t' do is point them out, then slide out o' the way. I can take care o' the rest."

"Yes, sir, I understand."

Longarm sat with his legs crossed and his Winchester laid over his lap. Petey perched in the rocking chair beside

170

Longarm's, his legs also crossed and his slide-action .22 across his lap exactly like Longarm held the Winchester.

Longarm angled his hat so the brim shielded his eyes from the rising sun. It occurred to him that he should buy Petey a wide-brimmed hat too. Maybe not anything as expensive as a beaver-felt Stetson, but maybe something in a nice-quality wool felt. He smiled. If the mercantile had anything like that in a small enough size.

After two cigars worth of sitting and watching—why was it that the dime novels never told the truth about how slow and boring keeping the peace could sometimes be— Longarm touched Petey on the elbow to draw his attention.

"Yes, sir?"

"Let's us walk over to the general store. It'll feel good t' stretch our legs." That was true enough. It was also true that Longarm could not get the idea of a hat for Petey out of his mind. It would make a nice surprise for the kid.

Petey hopped off his rocker and immediately draped his rifle over the crook of his arm. When this time Longarm chose to carry his Winchester at arm's length, holding it with his hand around the action, Petey shifted position and held his Lightning the same way. Longarm thought that was almost as funny as it was flattering.

Early as it was, there were some horses tied outside the saloon where Longarm had found his card game the night before.

He and Petey walked past the saloon, the scent of beer and sawdust sharp on the morning air, and entered the mercantile.

After a look around to make sure there were no customers who presented a threat, Longarm led the boy to the back of the store where there was a rack of cheap hats.

"How d' you think you'd look in one o' those, son?"

"Oh, those are grand, sir. They're real cowboy hats, aren't they? The really and true thing?"

"That they are. Would you like one?"

"If I can afford one someday, I sure would. Just like yours, sir."

"This bunch looks like mine, don't you think?"

"Yes, sir, they sure do."

"Then let's see if we can find one o' them to fit you."

"Oh, but I don't got any money."

"I do," Longarm said.

He thought Petey's jaw was going to drop clean off his face.

"I overheard what you gentlemen were saying," the proprietor put in. "If none of those fits, I have some more in my storeroom." He smiled. "With all of those to choose from and some wrapping paper to fold up narrow and slip inside the sweatband, I suspect we will be able to find one that works."

The gentleman was right about that, and young Peter Sanderson was wearing a proper cowboy hat—flat-crowned but in black rather than Longarm's snuff brown—when they walked out onto the street again.

Chapter 44

Crack! Crack! Crack!

The first Longarm knew there was trouble was the sharp crack and clatter of Petey's little .22 in rapid fire. The rifle barked and across the street a man standing outside the saloon covered his face with his hands and sank to his knees.

He was dead before Longarm reached him.

"What the hell was that about?" he snapped.

"That's the one they called Barncy," Petey said. "That's the one that took the clothes off my mama and . . . did things to her."

In all the time Longarm and the boy had been together, this was the first hint that Petey had actually seen his mother and sister raped. He had been holding it in all this time.

Well, now it was out. And in spades.

Longarm knelt beside the dead outlaw. The man had been hit once in the face, presumably Petey's first shot, and twice directly over the heart. It was no damned wonder he was dead.

"One thing I can say. You've learned to shoot mighty good."

"Where are the other ones, sir? I don't recognize any of these horses, so where are they now?"

Longarm stood and peered up and down the street. "They can't be awful far off."

According to Jim Freel, the morning bartender, Barney Lewis mentioned he only had time for a quick eye-opener. He was in town to pick up supplies.

"I got the impression that him and some others was camped somewhere out of town," Freel said. "If I remember correctly, he said something too about waiting for the next stage from Deadwood."

"Does the express line often carry gold on that run?" Longarm asked.

Freel nodded. "Right often."

Longarm thumbed his chin—he needed a shave but that would have to wait a little longer—and thought about what the kidnappers had been saying all along. They had a particular destination in mind and a particular stage to meet. A particularly heavy shipment of gold, which was most often and most sensibly shipped through the United States mail, would account for them being here now. They might well have advance knowledge of such a shipment.

If indeed that was their scheme. Their presence here could also be attributed to a hundred other plausible explanations too. For now, none of those were of concern. Right now, he only wanted to recover Petey's mother and/or sister.

Lordy, he just hoped they were alive after all this time.

"Did this Barney fella mention which direction his camp was?"

"No, and I'm afraid I didn't see which direction he came from."

"All right. Thanks."

Longarm stepped outside to where Petey was waiting. A group of townspeople was gathered around the dead outlaw's body. They were yapping like a bushel basket full of puppies; plenty of noise but no direction. Eventually, someone would take charge and see to a burying, he figured. In the meantime, he had more pressing matters to tend.

"C'mon, son. We need t' get the horses an' make a circle out around. Did you reload your rifle?"

"Yes, sir, I did."

Longarm paused for a moment. "What you did this morning, that was good shooting. I won't fault you for any of it an' I don't want you should feel bad about anything." He smiled. "But I do kinda wish you had gutshot him instead so's he could answer some questions before he died."

In all seriousness Petey asked, "Should I shoot them in the stomach next time then?"

"Jesus! No, I was funning you, boy. I hope there ain't a next time. That's what I'm here t' take care of. Now let's get our horses an' see if we can spot these jaspers. The rest of 'em seem to be back in camp waitin' for their eatables to be brought."

"Yes, sir." Petey broke into a trot to keep up with Longarm's quickened stride.

Chapter 45

"There," Longarm said. "That has t' be them."

The camp he was pointing to was well sited. The kidnappers—assuming they indeed were the ones who were squatting there—had set up with a sheer bluff at their backs, a stony creek bed in front, and wide-open grass to either side. It was possible to approach them from almost any direction . . . but impossible to do it without being seen.

"It's too far t' make out much about the people, but I see four. All o' them men, it looks like." He frowned. "This might not be our boys after all, Petey." Not for the first time, Longarm wished he had field glasses with him.

There was no point in wishing for some to drop down from the sky, however. He could have bought some in town when he had the chance, but he'd just never thought about it there.

Longarm sat atop the bay for a few moments, looking at the open terrain and the distant camp. The horse snorted and tossed its head, but he kept a tight rein on it.

He and Petey had been sitting there in plain sight for several minutes now. They almost had to have been seen by whoever was in that camp.

"I tell you what," Longarm said, "you and me are gonna put on a show for those boys. Are you game?"

"Yes, sir. I'll do whatever you say."

"All right then. Here's what we are fixing t' do."

Petey's pinto loped off to the north and was quickly out of sight. Longarm followed the shallow creek to the shady copse where the kidnappers' camp was.

He rode straight to them and stopped at the edge of their camp. They looked like they were set up to stay there awhile.

Up close, he could see that there were three men.

And one grown woman.

Longarm had expected to see the girl Betty. She was young. She was said to be pretty. She was not here.

This woman was either Petey's mother, Agnes Sanderson, or he had the wrong outfit here.

Longarm let his reins go slack and reached up to thumb his hat back on his head. He took out a cigar and lit it, then with the cheroot clenched between his teeth said, "Good mornin', gents. Might I ask if you'all have seen a pair o' black cows and a spotted calf pass by this way?"

"Lost some, did you?" The man asking the question was a tall, lanky fellow. Like the others, he was heeled. He did not, however, have his pistol in hand and gave no indication that he intended to use it. All three of the men seemed relaxed.

"We surely did. Damn things got away during the night. We'll get 'em, though."

"We?"

"Me an' my boy George."

"That was him you were riding with when you came over that rise?"

"That's right. I told him to make a circle around an' drive them back toward me if he sees them." Longarm grinned. "His bones ain't so brittle as mine of a morning. Let him do some of the work, right?"

178

"Yeah. Right. Sorry, mister, but we've not seen no cows, black or otherwise. But if we do see them, we'll sure enough hold them for you."

"That's mighty kind o' you." Longarm stretched and groaned. "Say, could I borrow a cup o' coffee there? That stuff smells awful good."

"Sure thing. Step down. Alva, hand this gentleman a cup so he can have a little dab of coffee, will you?"

Alva. There couldn't be very many people in this part of the country carrying that name. Alva White was one of the kidnappers.

Which meant that the tall fellow, the leader of the pack, was almost certainly Raymond Danaher. And with Barney dead, that would make the last one standing over there by the fire Charles "Chuck" Hill.

The woman . . . maybe it was Mrs. Sanderson. Hell, maybe they had kidnapped another female in these last few days.

Longarm dismounted and led his bay to the picket rope the kidnappers had strung. In truth, these boys put together a pretty decent camp. Comfortable. But then they spent an unusual amount of time out away from civilization. He tied the bay at the end of the line and walked back toward the fire.

The woman, who had not yet spoken a word, was squatting there with a cup of steaming coffee in her hand ready to give to Longarm.

Petey was off on a wild-goose chase. The woman was down low and about as out of the way as she was likely to get.

It seemed time.

"Boys," Longarm said, "I happen t' be a United States marsh—"

That was as far as he got before all hell broke loose.

Chapter 46

Danaher and White went for their guns before Longarm could finish getting the words out of his mouth to announce himself as the marshal he was. Hill seemed somewhat slower when it came to thinking.

Danaher cleared leather quickly, but it was obvious that he had worked on his speed to the exclusion of accuracy. His .45 spat lead and smoke in a hurry, but the bullet did not come anywhere near Longarm.

Longarm's Colt was half a heartbeat slower. But his bullet flew true.

Danaher went down with his throat ripped out and blood spraying half a dozen feet into the air.

Alva White screamed and clutched at his eyes as a cup of boiling hot coffee hit him in the face.

Hill inexplicably doubled over as if he had a sudden belly cramp. An instant afterward, Longarm heard the sharp snap of Petey's .22. The kid had ignored Longarm's instructions to circle around, and instead was up there on top of the bluff shooting down at these men who had disrupted a happy family life.

And Longarm had advised him to gutshoot the bastards. He had not *meant* it. But he had sure as hell said it.

"You bitch," Alva White screamed as he staggered past the fire trying to reach the woman.

White raised his revolver. The gun was cocked. Longarm had to assume that White intended to shoot his captive for the audacity of distracting him with the steaming-hot coffee. Then White pointed the gun at the woman.

Before he had time enough to pull the trigger, though, he went down. With *two* bullets in him. One from Longarm's Colt and the other from Petey's .22.

Longarm checked to make sure Danaher and White were dead, then took Chuck Hill's pistol from him. Not that Hill was interested in causing any more trouble. His focus at the moment was on his belly. And on the fact that he was dying. Still, it seemed a good idea to disarm him, just to make sure.

Then Longarm walked over to the lady and took his hat off. "May I ask your name, ma'am?"

"Sanderson," she said. "Agnes Sanderson. These . . . these animals killed the rest of my family. Murdered them in cold blood, my husband, my daughter, my son . . . everyone."

Longarm smiled. "Not quite everyone, ma'am. That was Petey up top o' the bluff shooting down a minute ago. I expect he's back on his horse an' headed this way by now. But what about the girl? What about Betty? An' what for was these fellows up here anyway?"

"Betty . . . I hate to say this about it, really I do, but Betty whined. She cried all the time and annoyed them. I told her to do whatever they wanted, that our first task was to survive, but she didn't listen. They finally got so tired of hearing her complain that they killed her. It was . . . ugly. Very ugly the way they did it. I buried her"—Mrs. Sanderson motioned vaguely toward the southeast—"somewhere back there. I don't know where it was. I couldn't begin to take you to it. Nor to the place where my husband and son were killed."

"You wasn't paying attention, ma'am. Petey is alive. He's just fine. He'll be here in a few minutes. I reckon it's safe t' say that he'll be glad to see you. Before I came along, he was heading out on his own t' find you an' rescue you. That is one awful brave little boy." Longarm smiled and pointed. "There, ma'am. Look there. Here he comes."

Longarm stepped back and left mother and son to their reunion, albeit one whose joy was tinged with sadness.

Watch for

**LONGARM AND THE
DIABLO GOLD**

the 354th novel in the exciting LONGARM
series from Jove

Coming in May!

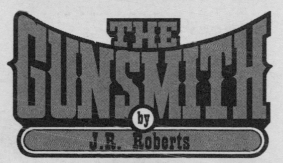